"You're actually a pretty great guy, Neil Hamilton…"

I used to be. Neil wanted to tell Maggie that. For some reason, he wanted this woman to know that once upon a time he had been a different kind of guy.

The sort of guy she would have liked.

Instead he said, "That probably just proves you don't know me any better than Oliver does."

"Well, I'll tell you what I do know. You've been an answer to prayer for me tonight, and I'm thankful."

An answer to prayer. He flinched, and Oliver stirred in his sleep and made a fussy noise.

"Maybe we should stop talking," Neil murmured gruffly, "and let Oliver get deeply enough asleep so that you can take him back home."

"Oh," Maggie whispered with an embarrassed nod. "You're probably right. I'll shut up."

She kept looking at him, though, so Neil closed his eyes, hoping to discourage any further conversation.

If he got drawn into a discussion with Maggie about God, that would prove once and for all to her that he wasn't the great guy she thought he was…

Laurel Blount lives on a small farm in Middle Georgia with her husband, David, their four children, a milk cow, dairy goats, assorted chickens, an enormous dog, three spoiled cats and one extremely bossy goose with boundary issues. She divides her time between farm chores, homeschooling and writing, and she's happiest with a cup of steaming tea at her elbow and a good book in her hand.

Books by Laurel Blount

Love Inspired

A Family for the Farmer
A Baby for the Minister
Hometown Hope
A Rancher to Trust
Lost and Found Faith

Visit the Author Profile page at Harlequin.com.

Lost and Found Faith

Laurel Blount

LOVE INSPIRED
INSPIRATIONAL ROMANCE

LOVE INSPIRED®

INSPIRATIONAL ROMANCE

Recycling programs for this product may not exist in your area.

ISBN-13: 978-1-335-56721-5

Lost and Found Faith

Copyright © 2021 by Laurel Blount

This edition published by arrangement with Harlequin Books S.A.

For questions and comments about the quality of this book, please contact us at CustomerService@Harlequin.com.

Love Inspired
22 Adelaide St. West, 40th Floor
Toronto, Ontario M5H 4E3, Canada
www.Harlequin.com

Printed in U.S.A.

And whoso shall receive one such little child in my name receiveth me.
—*Matthew* 18:5

For the precious children who've joined
our family through adoption and foster care:
Joanna and Levi Blount, Michael and
Hayleigh Grace Hall, and others equally beloved.
You have blessed us beyond measure.

Acknowledgments

Special thanks to Leigh Hall and Clarissa Pipes,
who answered many questions regarding foster
care protocols. Any errors are entirely my own.

Chapter One

"Car keys aren't in here, either." Neil Hamilton pulled his head out of the clothes dryer and banged the metal door shut. He sat back on his heels and ran a hand through his hair. "That takes care of all the usual places. Where'd I leave them this time?"

"Meow." The skinny orange cat who'd taken up residence at the rented cabin thumped his striped tail against the laundry room floor.

He shot the animal a narrow glance. "I wasn't talking to you. I don't talk to cats."

At least, he never had. Of course, before this stray had turned up last week, he'd never fed one or let one in the house, either.

He glanced at his watch and winced. This cabin was perched on the outskirts of Cedar Ridge, Georgia, and the drive down the mountain to the high school took exactly eighteen minutes. If he didn't leave soon, he'd be late for his meeting with Principal Audrey Aniston. She'd hinted that there was some issue with the summer school classes he was scheduled to teach, and Neil was determined to find out exactly what the problem was—and to solve it.

He was counting on those classes. Teaching history to hormone-distracted teenagers could be frustrating, but since the accident three years ago, his strict routine was the only thing that kept him sane. He had to teach summer school. Otherwise he'd have nine empty weeks stuck out here on this mountain with nothing to do but remember.

That wasn't an option. The two-week break he was suffering through now was bad enough.

Frustrated, Neil massaged his temples. His brain had won him all sorts of lofty academic awards, but it was worse than useless when it came to keeping track of keys. Or reading glasses or important papers or pretty much anything else.

Laura would've laughed at his predicament. *The absentminded professor. You're such a stereotype, Neil!* Then his late wife would have unearthed his keys in the vegetable crisper or some other unlikely spot and presented them to him with a kiss.

He jerked away from the thought as if he'd touched a hot stove and tried to focus.

Had he left the keys in his Jeep, maybe? He

hadn't considered that because he knew he'd have needed them to unlock the cabin. But, of course, if he'd forgotten to lock the front door—*again*—he might not have noticed.

His phone alarm beeped as he stepped out onto the front porch. He paused in the fragrant shade of the climbing summer roses to silence it. Leave for Meeting NOW flashed on the small screen. He fought the urge to throw the phone in the blooming bushes, shoving it back in his pocket instead.

When he looked up, a movement off to his right caught his eye. He glanced that way, expecting to see another white-tailed deer browsing along the tree line. He blinked and did a double take.

There was a little kid in his yard.

A tiny brown-haired boy dressed in red shorts and a striped T-shirt was hoisting himself onto the low rock wall that divided the yard of the original cabin from the rest of the centuries-old farm. No adult was in sight, and the kid couldn't have been more than, what—three, maybe? Neil wasn't all that good at assessing the ages of kids under twelve. Way too young to be off by himself, in any case.

How'd the boy even get here? After doing some research, Neil had chosen this cabin for its isolation. Sweet Springs Farm had been allowed to stay when the Chattahoochee National Forest was formed around it, so both the 1940s farmhouse and this original Sawyer cabin were bordered by nothing but trees and wildlife. Ruby Sawyer's farm was a brisk five-minute walk down the mountain, and as far as he knew, his elderly landlady lived alone.

The little boy teetered on the wall, and Neil flinched.

"Careful!" he called.

At the sound of Neil's voice, the child jerked his head in the direction of the house. The sudden movement made him lose his balance, and arms flailing, he plummeted off the side of the wall.

A heart-stopping second of silence was followed by an escalating scream. Neil sprinted down the worn stone steps and dropped to his knees beside the howling toddler.

"Are you hurt?" Wailing, the child nodded, his blue eyes shimmering with tears. "Where?" The little boy pointed to his knee, where an angry scrape was reddening with blood.

"Whoa! Ouch." Neil winced as the little boy yelled louder. "No, it's okay! We just need to clean it up and put a Band-Aid on it, that's all." He hoisted the child to his feet and gently brushed off the clinging bits of grass and debris.

As fat tears rolled down the child's flushed cheeks, Neil scanned the yard. Still no sign of a parent. "Somebody has to be looking for you. Where's your mom?"

The child only sobbed on, but now there was a more desperate tone to the cries. Neil's questions were making things worse.

What was he supposed to do here? The ruffled edge of a disposable diaper was peeking above the waistband of the kid's shorts. This little guy was barely more than a baby, and Neil worked with teenagers. Babies were way outside his skill set.

Maybe if things had worked out differently three years ago, if he hadn't forgotten his wallet that day…or if he hadn't asked Laura to drop it off at his school on her way to the ultrasound appointment… Neil shook his head to clear it of the regrets that never missed an opportunity to jab him.

Beat yourself up later, Hamilton. Right now you have to help this kid.

"Let's go inside, and I'll doctor that for you." He had two master's degrees. Surely, he could figure out how to patch up a skinned knee. "Then we'll figure out who you belong to."

The child was still crying, his face mottled red and wet with tears. His frightened eyes looked into Neil's for a long second, reminding Neil of the times he'd startled a deer or a squirrel around the cabin. They always looked at you like that for a heartbeat or two while they decided whether or not to bolt.

Finally, the little boy held up his hands, wiggling his fingers in a baby language so universal that even Neil could translate it.

Carry me.

He hesitated. Little kids weren't his specialty. He'd never picked one up in his life, but it couldn't be that hard, could it? He awkwardly hoisted the little boy up into his arms. To his relief, the child stopped screaming, hiccuped softly and laid his head against Neil's chest.

The kid's yelling must have scared away everything in a half-mile radius, because Neil heard none of the usual birdsong or animal rustlings, just the sound of the child's uneven breathing. Wispy hair tickled Neil's chin, and small fists gathered handfuls of his shirt as the toddler clamped on.

Neil's heart stirred with a mixture of sympathy and anger. Poor little guy. What kind of parent let a baby wander around by himself on the edge of a national forest?

He carried the child inside to the cabin's cramped bathroom. Once there, he rummaged one-handed through his disordered medicine cabinet, impatiently tossing four herbal remedies for sleeplessness into the trash can.

Might as well. The things didn't work anyway.

He finally unearthed a tube of antibiotic cream and a box of adhesive bandages. Balancing the toddler on the lip of the sink, he stuck a clean washcloth under the tap. He wrung it out and swabbed at the dirt and blood on the boy's knee.

The child yelped and shot Neil an accusing look.

"Sorry, buddy. I have to clean it, but I'll try to be more careful." He dabbed very lightly. "Better?"

The little boy didn't answer, but he didn't yelp again, either. He stuck one thumb in his mouth and watched solemnly as Neil finished cleaning the knee, applied the ointment and angled two bandages over the wide scrape.

"All done." Neil straightened and surveyed his work. Not bad for a total amateur. "You're a brave little guy, aren't you? What's your name?"

The child's sad eyes studied Neil. After a long pause, the little boy popped his wet thumb out of his mouth.

"Owiver."

"Owiver?" What kind of name was that? Neil puzzled over it for a minute before realization struck him. "Oh. Oliver? Like Oliver Twist?"

The little boy blinked at the literary reference, but he nodded. "Owiver." He looked at his knee, then back at Neil. "Fanks," he offered shyly.

Neil's brain must have booted up its baby-talk translator, because this time he understood. "You're welcome."

The child continued to look at him expectantly,

but Neil had no clue what he was supposed to do now that the knee had been taken care of. Didn't little kids usually get lollipops or something after incidents requiring Band-Aids? Neil had nothing like that on the premises. He had some chocolate-covered espresso beans, but he was pretty sure those weren't toddler friendly.

"Well," Neil said finally. "I guess we'd better find your mother. She must be worried about you."

Oliver didn't answer, but he broke his gaze away from Neil's and became suddenly interested in an unremarkable corner of the bathroom. The thumb went back in his mouth, and for a second, Neil thought the toddler was about to start crying again. A warning bell pinged in the back of Neil's brain.

Shouldn't a hurt kid *want* his mom?

"Oliver?" A muffled female voice called frantically from outside the house. "*Oliver!* Where are you? Answer me, sweetie! Please!"

"Looks like your mom found us." Neil watched Oliver's expression closely. The little boy tilted his head and glanced briefly in the direction of the woman's voice. Leaning forward on the sink, he buried his face in the front of Neil's shirt. The warning bell in Neil's mind pinged louder.

Even the teens he worked with wanted their

parents when they were sick or scared. This wasn't normal.

"Oliver!"

"Come on, buddy. I need to have a talk with your mother." Neil gathered the little boy into his arms. It was easier this time, and the child relaxed against his shoulder, thumb still in his mouth.

As he turned toward the door, Neil's glance caught on their reflection in the medicine-cabinet mirror. His glasses were slightly askew, there was a shadow of summer-break beard on his cheeks, and his dark hair was rumpled because he'd forgotten to comb it before he'd discovered his keys were missing. Nothing unusual there.

But cradled in his arms was a tiny boy, bits of dead grass still scattered on the back of his shirt, cheeks flushed pink, sucking his thumb, his head settled trustingly in the niche between Neil's neck and his shoulder.

Now, that? Definitely unusual.

Something sharp and hard sliced through Neil's heart. *My life could've been like this. Laura and I were supposed to have a son. God, why didn't You—?*

He cut the thought short. He'd stopped asking God those questions years ago. What was the point?

"Come on," he repeated, patting the boy's back

with his free hand. "Let's go see what this is all about."

He opened the front door just as a red-haired woman enveloped in an oversize green chef's apron barreled up his front steps. She stopped so fast that she had to grab the rail to keep herself upright. She pressed her free hand over her heart and gasped.

"Oh, you've got him!" Relief washed over her pale face as her eyes fixed on the toddler in Neil's arms. "I've never been so glad to see anybody in my whole life! Oliver Johnston, you scared me and Grandma Ruby half to death! Honey, you *have* to stop running off like this."

The little boy's only response was to burrow closer against Neil's chest. Neil narrowed his eyes as he considered the woman in front of him.

She was vibrantly pretty, in a flushed, disheveled sort of way. Her ruddy hair was pinned up in a haphazard bun that was slipping apart, and long strands had drooped to curl beside her left cheek. Her eyes were as green as the first spring leaves, and golden freckles spattered across the bridge of her nose. She was petite but not skeletally thin, and she favored eye-popping colors. Underneath the huge apron peeked bright purple short sleeves embellished with multicolored cupcakes.

She smelled like freshly baked cookies.

This was a kindergarten-teacher sort of woman,

the kind of person he'd assume kids would be drawn to like ants to sugar, but Oliver sure didn't seem fond of her.

"Who are you, exactly?" Neil asked bluntly.

"Oh! Sorry!" The woman had a generous mouth, and when she smiled, it seemed like the afternoon sun had brightened a few extra watts. "I'm so relieved that I forgot to introduce myself. Maggie Byrne." She took her fingers off her chest, revealing Angelo's scrawled in flowing white script across her apron. She extended the hand in his direction. "I'm Ruby Sawyer's daughter. Oliver and I moved in with her about six weeks ago."

This was his new landlady's daughter? Neil's brain ticked over this information in a millisecond. And she worked at Angelo's. Some little bakery downtown, wasn't it? Yeah, the building with the pink-and-white-striped awnings and the white curlicued-metal furniture out front, always teeming with people.

He'd never been there. Not his kind of place.

After a second's hesitation, he accepted the woman's hand. Her fingers clasped his with a warm enthusiasm that made strange tingles run all the way up to his elbow. He released her hand as fast as he could, and she tilted her head, regarding him with a friendly curiosity.

"You must be Ruby's new renter. Neil…"

"Hamilton."

"Right. It's nice to finally meet you in person."

"You're Mrs. Sawyer's daughter?" Strange, then, that she kept calling his landlady by her first name. Folks in the Blue Ridge Mountains of Georgia trended toward the traditional.

The relationship also seemed biologically unlikely. The two women looked nothing alike. This woman was all rosy color and curves, and Mrs. Sawyer was sallow and spare framed.

"I am." She made a point of looking him straight in the eye as she answered.

Neil had worked with teenagers long enough to know when somebody wasn't telling him the whole truth. Not that it mattered. This woman's specific relationship to Mrs. Sawyer wasn't his immediate concern. "Is he—" he nodded down at Oliver's head "—yours?"

"You mean is he my son? Yes, he is. Or rather, he will be really soon. I'm adopting him. He's going to live with Grandma Ruby and me, and the three of us are going to be a family. Aren't we, Oliver?"

Neil narrowed his eyes. There it was again—that note of not-quite-the-truth.

Maggie nibbled on her lip as she studied the toddler. "Is he okay, do you think? He…uh…doesn't usually like to be held."

"All I saw was a skinned knee. I'm no doctor, but I think he's all right."

"That's a relief!" Maggie fished a cell phone out of her pocket. "I'd better let Ruby know Oliver's safe and sound." She kept her eyes fixed on the boy as she waited for an answer, as if she were afraid he was going to disappear again. "Ruby? I've found him over here at the cabin. No, he's just fine, thankfully. You wait there. We'll be home in a few minutes."

She ended the call and flashed a smile at Neil before turning her attention back to the boy. "Let's go home and tell Grandma Ruby you're okay. Maybe we'll all have a glass of milk and a cookie. How does that sound?" Maggie held out her hands, but Oliver snuffled against Neil's shirt and shook his head.

Disappointment flickered in Maggie's eyes, but she kept her arms outstretched. "Sorry," she murmured, darting a glance at Neil. "He's only been with me for about a month, and we're still working on attachment. But we'll get there, won't we, Oliver? Thanks so much for your help, Neil. You've saved the day, you really have. Now, I'm sure you have things to do, so we'd better get going."

That was his cue to hand Oliver over. As if sensing Neil's thoughts, the little boy clamped on tighter.

"I could carry him back to Mrs. Sawyer's for you," Neil heard himself volunteering. "His knee was banged up pretty good, and I think he's still upset."

"Poor little guy." Maggie craned her neck to inspect his knees, zeroing in on the injured one. "Looks like you've administered some top-quality first aid." As she angled Oliver's leg for a better look, her fingers brushed against Neil's chest.

He jumped as if he'd been shocked, and she lifted surprised eyes to his. "I'm sorry! Did I poke you? Look, it's kind of you to offer to walk back with us, but I don't want to put you to any more trouble. You look like you're all dressed up to go somewhere."

The meeting. He glanced at his watch and bit back a groan.

It was too late to get to the high school, so he might as well see this little drama through. He'd reschedule with Principal Aniston later.

"I'm not going anywhere. Not now, anyway. I'll carry him."

Maggie smiled. "Well, okay. Thanks."

He edged past her down the cabin's worn steps.

"Neil?"

He turned. "What?"

"Would you like me to grab these for you?"

She pointed to his keys, dangling from the

dented doorknob. He blew out a weary breath. "Just leave them. Thanks."

Then maybe when he got back home, he'd be able to find them.

Maybe.

When Ruby had fretted over her new renter being such a "sad, quiet fellow," Maggie hadn't paid much attention. Most likely this Neil guy just wasn't responding to Ruby's firehose brand of neighborliness. Some folks didn't. Maggie loved Ruby beyond all reason, but she knew her blunt-spoken foster mom could be an acquired taste.

But now that she'd met him… Maggie sneaked a sideways glance at the man walking silently beside her. Ruby might be getting older, but her instincts about people were as good as ever.

A story of hurt was written all over Neil's face. It was in his eyes, in the tense lines around his mouth and even in the stiff, slightly awkward way he carried Oliver. Maggie had a few instincts of her own, and they told her Neil Hamilton's misery wasn't fresh. His pain had settled in to stay, like a long spell of dreary winter weather.

That was too bad. Maggie sighed as she side-stepped one of the many tree roots snaking across the red clay path. While waiting on customers at Angelo's, she saw plenty of troubled folks, and she always wished she had more ability to help them.

Unfortunately, most of the time all she could do was sympathize—and maybe plop an extra cookie in their bag if Angelo happened to be in a good mood.

She prayed for them, too, of course. She kept a little notebook of prayer concerns right next to her order pad in her apron pocket, and it was a slow day when she didn't add at least three new ones. She did what she could. It just never felt like enough, not when she knew firsthand what kind of unhappiness existed in the world. That was why she was so thankful for the opportunity to help Oliver.

If only he'd let her.

She looked at the little boy nestled in the man's arms. Oliver had never cuddled against her like that, not once. When Maggie picked him up, he held himself stiff as a board, his little hands placed against her chest, pushing her away. Or worse, he screamed at the top of his lungs. It broke her heart every time, even though Ruby promised Oliver would eventually learn to trust her.

So far, she'd seen no sign of that happening. She cut another glance at her companion, wondering what it was about this particular guy that had broken through Oliver's defenses.

At first glance, she didn't see anything obvious. Of course, even with that unapproachable expression on his face, Neil was no slouch in the looks department. Tall and lean, he had nice shoulders and thick dark brown hair that didn't look as if it had seen a comb recently.

He also sported a shadowy scruff of beard, but Maggie wondered if that was intentional or if he just hadn't bothered to shave lately. She kind of liked the casual, tousled look. She'd never been a big fan of men who spent a lot of time in front of mirrors.

But none of that was likely to matter much to Oliver—or to her, either. She'd take as many friends as the good Lord saw fit to give her, but she wasn't interested in romance. Maggie had witnessed one relationship disaster after another growing up, each one worse than the last. Now that Oliver had come into her life, she was determined to stay peacefully single, just like Ruby, and build a family by offering a home to children who needed one.

As if sensing her scrutiny, Neil glanced at her, his brown eyes cool and impersonal behind his rimless glasses. He turned his gaze forward again without speaking.

So that was the way he was going to play it. Stern and silent. Maggie's lips twitched. Working at the bakery had given her plenty of experience dealing with all kinds of people. As Angelo had gotten older and grouchier, he preferred to hide in the kitchen, leaving Maggie to cope with the customers. Maggie prided herself on being able to connect with pretty much anybody, and she viewed the surliest folks as a personal challenge.

Neil didn't know who he was up against.

"It's a good little hike, isn't it?" she observed cheerfully. "No wonder Oliver's zonked out."

"What?" He threw a concerned look at the slack-jawed toddler dozing in his arms. "He's fallen asleep. I don't think he hit his head when he fell, but I can't be sure."

"I don't think we need to worry. It's his nap time, and he walked a long way. I expect he's just worn-out, but I'll keep a close eye on him. So, Ruby told me you teach over at Cedar Ridge High?"

He hesitated briefly before answering. "Yes."

"That's a great school. I graduated from there myself." She waited, but he didn't pick up the ball. She tried again. "What subject do you teach?"

"History."

"History? Ew." Maggie hurried to bend the sagging branch of an oak sapling out of Neil's way.

He shot her a sharp glance as he passed. She met it innocently. *"Ew?"* he repeated.

Maggie smothered a smile. Sometimes you had to poke the silent ones a little to get them going. Once they started talking, things got easier.

"Sorry. History wasn't my favorite class. It was all dead folks and dates, you know?"

His eyebrows arched all the way above his glasses. The man had amazing eyes, Maggie decided, autumn-leaf brown with little golden flecks.

"Dead folks and dates? That's all you think history amounts to?"

He didn't sound offended. He sounded curious, as if she were some sort of odd creature he'd never encountered before. She offered him another bright smile.

"Oh, I'm not saying history's not interesting, but wouldn't you rather be making it than reading about it? I've never seen much point in looking backwards."

"Haven't you?" Something in the way he said the words made the back of her neck tickle. It prickled in the same way whenever she clambered up on Sawyer's Knob to look over the breathtaking mountain vista.

Be very careful here, her instincts warned, so she answered softly.

"Well, the past's over and done with, isn't it? If it was bad, you can't change it, and if it was good, you can't relive it. The present's a lot more interesting. I think—"

"This is a long way for a kid to walk by himself," Neil interrupted. "How long ago did you and your mother lose track of him?"

Maggie blinked. So much for trying to connect through some friendly banter. The teacherish disapproval in his tone made her feel like she'd just been caught peeking at somebody else's test paper.

Still, it was a valid question. She was worried, too. Oliver slipped away anytime they took their eyes off him, and he never answered when they called. Maggie had faithfully done all the attachment-fostering activities the social worker had recommended, but so far, Oliver showed no signs of settling in.

"I'm not sure. He must've slipped out the back door after Ruby put him down for his nap. She didn't realize he was missing until she went to check on him later. She called me at the bakery in a panic, and I came right over. We searched the house first, then the yard and the barns. I saw the path leading over your way, and I thought—"

"He could've been seriously hurt. There are hundreds of uninhabited acres behind this farm. If he'd strayed off the path, he could have died out there in the woods before anybody found him."

Maggie winced. Neil obviously didn't believe in mincing words, but she couldn't argue with his point.

"You're absolutely right," she agreed. "It's a dangerous area. Did you notice the marker we passed a few minutes back? It marks the trail leading out to Sawyer's Knob." He shook his head briefly, indicating that he had no idea what she was talking about. "It's an overlook, and the land around it's been eroding pretty badly over the last few years. If he'd turned that way—" She stopped short. She couldn't allow herself to think about that. "Trust me, I'm every bit as thankful for God's mercy today as you are."

Neil's face shifted, but he averted his eyes before she could read his expression. They walked the next few minutes in silence.

As the Sweet Springs farmhouse came into view, Maggie stopped in the middle of the path. "Hold up a second."

He halted a step ahead and turned, gently shifting Oliver in his arms. He was dappled with the dancing shadows of the summer leaves, but his face was grim. "What is it?"

"I understand you've got this whole righteous indignation thing going on, and I don't blame you. If I were standing outside this situation looking in, I'd probably feel just as outraged as you do. Fuss at me all you want, but please don't fuss at Ruby. She feels awful enough already. I promise you, I'll make sure this doesn't happen again."

"How?"

"Excuse me?"

"How are you going to make sure this doesn't happen again?"

Good question. "I don't know yet, but I'll figure it out."

A muscle jumped in Neil's jaw. "Miss Byrne—"

"Call me Maggie. Please."

He sighed. "Maggie, as a teacher, I'm a mandated reporter. That means that if I suspect any instance of child abuse or neglect—"

"I know what a mandated reporter is." She tried to hide her alarm. She ought to know. She'd been the subject of more than one teacher's report herself, growing up.

"—I'm required by law to report it," Neil finished as if she hadn't spoken.

"I appreciate your concern, but you're actually not mandated to report anything here." He looked skeptical, but her childhood had given her life's equivalent of a PhD in child-welfare laws. "Oliver is well-fed, clean and cared for. He's struggling to adjust to a new placement, and he wandered off when his caregiver thought he was napping. This is nothing but an accident."

"An accident that we both agree could have turned into a tragedy." Neil gazed down at the toddler asleep in his arms, and Maggie studied the change in his expression. A second ago, he'd come across as judgmental. Now he seemed only worried.

Her alarm ebbed. She couldn't fault any man for stepping up to protect a helpless child. She wished she'd had someone like Neil looking out for her when she'd been Oliver's age.

Her childhood might have gone a lot better if she had.

"I have to figure out the details, but you have my word that I'll tend to this. Oliver won't turn up on your doorstep again." Maggie's gaze lingered on the child cuddled against Neil's chest. Even in his sleep, his fingers gripped the fabric of Neil's shirt. Again, she felt that pinprick of envy. "He's taken to you like a duck takes to water, hasn't he? Why don't you come inside, and—"

Neil looked uncomfortable. "Thanks, but I'd better get back to the cabin."

"Oh, but Ruby will want to thank you, too. And—"

"I'm glad I could help. But, please understand, if this child—or any other child under your care—shows up in my yard again unsupervised, I'll be on the phone to the police. And next time, no amount of pretty-girl-next-door charm will talk me out of it. Is that clear?"

Maggie inhaled a slow, calming breath before she answered. "Perfectly clear, yes." She held out her hands, and Neil carefully transferred Oliver into her embrace. Fortunately, the little boy was so deeply asleep that he barely stirred.

For a second after Oliver was out of his arms, Neil stayed where he was, so close that Maggie could smell his scent—laundry detergent mixed with a spicy man-shampoo. His eyes stayed fixed on Oliver, and after a brief hesitation, he reached out and smoothed a lock of hair that had fallen over the little boy's forehead.

Then Neil seemed to come to himself, and he looked sharply at Maggie. "Please take better care of him."

She nodded without speaking, and he held her eyes for a long heartbeat. Then he turned on his heel and stalked back up the path through the woods.

Maggie waited until he'd vanished into the trees before resuming her trek toward the farmhouse. Ruby would be overjoyed to see Oliver safe and sound, and Maggie couldn't wait to tell her about the toddler's uncharacteristic response to Neil. Maybe it would help them figure out a new plan to connect with this traumatized little boy.

Or at the very least find some way to keep him from running away until he learned to trust them.

That might be tough since at the moment Maggie's brain only seemed able to focus on one totally silly detail.

Stern, sad-eyed Neil Hamilton thought she was pretty.

Chapter Two

"Stop pacing, Maggie." Ruby patted the ladder-back chair beside hers at the kitchen table. "We both need to sit a spell and count our blessings. Oliver's safe in his bed, and everything's fine."

She sounded as if she were trying to convince herself as much as Maggie. The older woman's age-spotted hands still trembled, and her face was paper white. It took a good bit to rattle Ruby Sawyer, but Oliver's vanishing act had done it.

Maggie frowned. "Are you feeling all right, Ruby? Maybe I should call Logan and have him check you out. He's had all kinds of medical training since he went to work at the sheriff's department. We might as well put it to good use."

Ruby shook her head. "Don't you bother your brother. Besides, if you call Logan, he'll call everybody else, and they'll all come running out here lickety-split. Then we really *will* have ourselves a mess."

Ruby was right. Of her six children, only Logan and Maggie had settled in Cedar Ridge, but the others stayed in close touch. If her flock of grown-up foster kids thought anything was amiss with their mom, every one of them would drop what they were doing and converge on this weather-beaten house like a swarm of anxious bees. Ruby had suffered more than one health scare over the past couple of years, and everybody was worried about her.

None of them wanted to imagine a world without Ruby.

"I'll perk back up in a minute or two," Ruby continued. "When I went to peep in on that baby and he wasn't in his bed, my blood ran ice-cold. It gave me a turn, that's all."

Maggie bit her lip. "Maybe it's asking too much of you, having you foster Oliver until I can get licensed myself. I'm sorry. I didn't expect it to be so hard."

"Don't be silly. My house is open for any little'un who needs a safe place to stay, and it will be as long as I'm drawing breath. Anyway, this ain't nothing I haven't seen before. You children gave me plenty of gray hairs, too, but you all came around in the end."

"Really?" Maggie heard the desperation in her own voice. "Do you truly think Oliver's going to adjust like the rest of us did, Ruby?"

"I sure do. In God's own time." Ruby placed a work-roughened hand over Maggie's. "Oliver's had a heaping helping of pain, honey, losing his mama like he did, so unexpected. And from what his social worker's told us, that's not the half of what that poor baby's been through. Addicts get too caught up in their own troubles to take good care of their children. You know that yourself."

Maggie nodded. Yes, she did know, all too well.

"We just got to be patient and wait on God to heal his heart. It'll happen, sure as the world, but you can't rush it."

"I hope you're right."

"I am. Don't you worry. One day our little Oliver will run right into your arms and hug your neck. You'll see. Besides," Ruby continued, "going by what you told me, he turned a corner today. Somehow or another, Neil Hamilton got through to that baby." The older woman clucked her tongue thoughtfully. "You never know who the Lord's gonna use, do you?"

"I couldn't believe my eyes when I saw Oliver hanging on to him. I've been trying for weeks and getting nowhere. Maybe it's just *me* he can't stand."

Ruby cackled. "You? Well, if that ain't the silliest thing I've ever heard! Everybody loves you."

"Oliver doesn't. I'm worried, Ruby. I want to adopt him more than anything in this world, but maybe the social worker has a point. Maybe it's not fair for me to move forward if he's not able to attach to me."

"Nonsense." Ruby's fingers tightened over Maggie's. "Didn't nobody else want that child before you stepped up. Only three foster homes left open in this whole county, not counting mine, and not one of them would take a preschooler who's not potty-trained. That baby needs you. He'll figure that out sooner or later."

Maggie nodded. Her throat was too thick with tears to speak. Ruby always had a way of cutting to the heart of things.

"He's putting you through your paces, but you'll connect with him sooner or later because you ain't gonna give up. You got plenty of gumption, like all my kids. You make me proud, every one of you."

Maggie squeezed her foster mother's thin fingers. Ruby lavished love and approval on her kids as generously as she lavished butter on her homemade bread.

"You're right, Ruby. I'm not going to give up."

"Good." The older woman scooted back her chair to retrieve a white bakery box from the chipped countertop. "I expect you'd best get to work before Angelo has one of his fits. Before you do, you can drop these peanut butter cookies you brought home off at Neil's house as a thank-you for rescuing Oliver. And then, once you've got him good and buttered up, sit him down and ask him exactly what he did that made Oliver take to him so. Maybe it's something you can copy."

Maggie shook her head, alarmed. "I'm not sure that's a good idea. Neil seems like a very private person. I think I've intruded on his life enough for one day. Don't you?"

"Not if you're bringing him cookies." Ruby nudged the box in Maggie's direction. "Any man who lives by himself is always glad to get something good to eat." She cut the younger woman a meaningful glance. "In case you didn't happen to notice, Neil ain't married."

Maggie sighed. Ruby was a relentless matchmaker, always angling to find somebody special for her beloved fosterlings. She hadn't succeeded yet; their family histories were so full of hurt that each of them was cautious in relationships.

That hadn't stopped Ruby from trying.

"Not interested."

"Why not? Ain't he handsome enough?"

Maggie's memory presented her with a picture of Neil walking down the red clay mountain path, a little boy cradled in his arms. "Well, sure. I guess. But I'm not looking."

"None of you children are," Ruby retorted. "That's why I'm looking for you. I'd like to see all of you settled down with families of your own before I go to glory."

"Well, you're wasting your time on me." Maggie patted her mom's hand. "I plan to be a strong, single mom, just like you."

Ruby made a face. "You can do a sight better than *that*. I ain't nothing special."

I ain't nothing special.

Those were some of the first words Ruby Sawyer had said to Maggie when she'd arrived at Sweet Springs Farm as a twelve-year-old, hard-to-place foster child.

They'd been standing in this very kitchen. Maggie had just been thrown out of her latest home when the scrupulously neat foster mom had discovered Maggie's secret cache of hoarded food in the back of the bedroom closet, swarming with bugs.

On the drive over, her frustrated social worker had made herself very clear. This placement was Maggie's last chance. If she didn't stop stealing food, her next stop would be the group home four counties over, and no kid in her right mind wanted to go there.

The trouble was, Maggie didn't think she *could* stop. She'd gone hungry too many times, and now she never felt safe unless she had a stockpile of food tucked away. So she'd ducked her head and resigned herself to going to the group home sooner rather than later.

Her caseworker had marched her into the old farmhouse kitchen. Ruby had stood, smoothed the faded apron tied around her skinny waist and adjusted her smudged bifocals. In typical Ruby fashion, she hadn't wasted time passing pleasantries. She'd brushed aside the social worker's introductions and gotten down to business.

"Baby, you been lots of places, I know. Likely some folks have treated you bad, but that ain't gonna happen here. I ain't nothing special, but I never lie. I'll never give up on you, neither. Long story short, you're my girl now, Maggie Byrne, and I'm going to love you as long as I'm breathing. You got my word on that."

Such simple words spoken by a scrawny old lady she'd never seen before in her life. Still, something about the no-nonsense note in Ruby's voice had made the aching knot in the pit of Maggie's stomach unravel. To Maggie's embarrassment, she'd started to ugly cry right there in the shabby kitchen.

Maggie hadn't cried for years, and she never let people touch her. But she hadn't protested when Ruby had gathered her into a hard hug.

The woman had smelled like chocolate cake and sun-dried laundry, and she'd gently rubbed Maggie's heaving back. "That's right, child. Let it all out and be done with it. Old Ruby's got you now. Everything's gonna be all right."

Maggie still remembered how safe she'd felt in Ruby's embrace. That feeling was exactly what she wanted to give to Oliver. And she'd find some way to do that, sooner or later, because she'd had the best possible teacher.

"I think you're very special, Ruby. All of us do."

A soft, maternal warmth sparkled in Ruby's faded hazel eyes. "And that right there's the joy of my life, baby girl. All right, we've sat here jawing long enough! Here." Ruby pushed the bakery box into Maggie's hands. "Give Neil my best, you hear? And don't forget. Feed him one of these cookies before you start asking him questions. That'll soften him up just fine."

While she spoke, Ruby opened the screen door and hustled Maggie toward the steps with a firm hand on the small of her back. "Now, get on with you, and I'll see you this evening."

The screen door slammed. Maggie found herself standing in the backyard, Ruby's chickens and milk goat watching her hopefully from behind their wooden fences.

"I've just been railroaded," she observed aloud.

She didn't want to go back to the cabin.

She'd found a lot to like about Neil. He was kind and gentle with Oliver, and yet he had a stern fierceness about him when it came to doing the right thing. Maggie admired that; she really did. Maybe a little too much.

Because back on the trail when she'd made her silly quip about the past, there'd been something in Neil's eyes that had sent up warning flares deep in her stomach. This man's pain, whatever it was, ran deep. Maggie knew firsthand what that kind of pain did to people, how it caused them to hurt others, even when they honestly didn't mean to. She did her best to help people, sure, but except for her foster family, she'd learned to keep her heart carefully guarded from them, too. She cultivated light, breezy friendships, but that was it.

There was nothing breezy about Neil Hamilton.

And yet somehow he'd managed to connect with Oliver in a way Maggie couldn't. Her mind flicked to the concerned look on Mrs. Darnell's face during her last home visit, to her carefully worded warnings about what this lack of attachment might mean for Oliver's adoption if it continued. She'd suggested that the child might be more open to bonding with a father figure, that a two-parent family might be the wiser option.

There weren't any two-parent foster families available right now, though, and anyway, Maggie wasn't going to give up. She'd find some way to connect with the little boy.

But maybe she *should* ask Neil a few questions. At this point, she needed all the help she could get, and she owed it to Oliver not to leave any stone unturned.

Maggie drew in a deep breath and squeezed her eyes shut.

Okay, God. I'm going to give this a try. Please help me find some way to get this man to talk to me and show me whatever it is about him that spoke to Oliver. Amen.

She started up the trail leading to the cabin, tucking the bakery box carefully under one arm. Ruby had a good point about the cookies. Maggie had used them to smooth over more than one ticklish situation.

She sure hoped Neil had a sweet tooth.

"I'm sorry, Neil. All the summer school positions are filled." Principal Audrey Aniston's voice came clearly through the speaker on the phone Neil had propped on his desk.

His heart sank to his shoes. "Again, I'm really sorry about missing our meeting. There was—"

"—an emergency. I know. That has nothing to do with my decision not to put you on the roster."

"Then I don't understand. When I took this job, you agreed that I'd have a standing position on the summer school staff."

"I know. That's what our meeting today was

for—to explain why I feel it's necessary to adjust that."

"Explain it now." A tinkling chime of electronic music made Neil glance around the room, puzzled. What was that noise? He refocused his attention on the conversation. He had to get this straightened out. Immediately.

The veteran educator cleared her throat. "I'd prefer to have this conversation face-to-face."

That didn't sound encouraging. The chime trilled again, but he ignored it. "In that case, I can reschedule for any time this week that works for you."

"That's the problem." Neil heard planner pages flipping. "My schedule's jam-packed for the next few weeks. I don't—" The principal paused as the chiming started again, followed by a series of thumps coming from the front porch. "Neil, is somebody at your door?"

So that was what all that noise was. A doorbell. He hadn't even realized this ancient cabin had a doorbell. "I guess so. Hold on a second."

He scooped up his phone, walked through the living room and opened the door.

The cool wind that always blew off the hazy blue-green mountains rushed into the living room, scattering his papers and wafting in an unexpected aroma of peanut butter cookies. The woman from this morning stood on the porch, her red hair tousled by the breeze, a glossy white box clutched in her hands.

Her bright smile hit him like a second rush of unsettling air. "Hi! Remember me? Maggie Byrne, Oliver's mom. Do you have a minute to talk? Oh—sorry!" She gestured to the phone in his hand. "Am I interrupting?"

Principal Aniston answered before he could. "Maggie? Audrey here. I've been meaning to call you. Those chocolate mint cupcakes you made for my secretary's retirement party were divine. Thank you so much!"

Maggie's face lit up, and she leaned closer to the phone. "You're welcome, Audrey! I'm working on the sugar-free cake recipes for your sister's sixtieth birthday bash, too. I'll have the samples ready for you to try on Thursday, just like we planned."

"You're an absolute doll, Maggie! Lisa's so sick of her diabetic diet. The woman's impossible to buy for, but a birthday cake from Angelo's she could actually eat? She'll love it!"

Maggie's laugh reminded Neil of the stubborn bird that warbled joyfully outside his bedroom window at dawn each morning. "Lisa was our best customer before Dr. Maynard put her on that diet." She glanced at Neil. "Sorry, I didn't mean to hijack your conversation with Mr. Hamilton."

"Oh, no. We're done," Principal Aniston assured her. "I'll give you a call in a couple weeks, Neil, and we'll set up a meeting."

He couldn't wait that long. He thought fast. "Why don't I come by the bakery on Thursday? We can talk while you taste those cakes." He wasn't crazy about having this discussion in a public place, but he couldn't afford to be picky.

He needed to get to the bottom of this.

"You want to meet at Angelo's? I don't know…"

Maggie shot him a sharp look, then leaned back toward the phone. "That's a great idea, Audrey! It never hurts to have a second opinion."

There was a short silence on the other end of the phone. "I guess it would be good to go ahead and get this dealt with. Be at Angelo's on Thursday at one o'clock. We'll have a short sit-down. And, Neil? Be nice to Maggie, okay? She's a real gem."

Maggie's musical laugh bubbled again. "Thanks, Audrey."

"Anytime, sweet girl." There was a click as the call disconnected.

"Sorry about butting in." Cute dimples dented Maggie's cheeks on either side of an apologetic smile. "Audrey and I are old friends. May I come in?"

"Oh." He blinked. "Sure." He stepped back from the doorway, and she looked around the small living room with interest.

"I haven't been inside this cabin since I helped Ruby clean it after Mrs. Carter moved to Arizona to live with her daughter. You've been here a couple of months, right?"

"Right."

"Well, now that you're on summer break, you'll have time to get the rest of your stuff unpacked and really make the space your own."

Neil scanned the room, puzzled. What was she talking about? He'd already unpacked everything that mattered. He'd dispatched with that chore his first evening here.

It hadn't taken long. All the necessary furniture had come with the rental. This room offered a leather sofa, a matching recliner, a desk and two floor-to-ceiling bookcases bracketing a riverstone fireplace. Except for repositioning the writing desk away from a big window that looked out over the mountains—too distracting—he hadn't seen much point in rearranging. He'd unboxed his reference books, plugged in his laptop and considered himself settled.

"Oh, look! Rover's here!" Maggie crouched, wiggling her fingers at the orange stray who'd wandered in from the bedroom. The cat scampered to her and arched his back against her stroking hand. "Ruby's been worrying, you little stinker!"

"This cat belongs to Mrs. Sawyer?" Good, Neil told himself sternly. He did not need a cat.

He didn't.

"Oh, no." Maggie smiled up at him. "Rover's a free spirit. He just appeared at the farm one day, and he comes and goes as he pleases. Ruby wondered why he hasn't shown up to eat for the last few days." The cat crossed the room to rub against Neil's slacks, and Maggie rose to her feet. "You're welcome to keep him. He'll be good company for you."

Neil started to tell her that she could take the cat right back home with her. He didn't need company, and even if he did, he wouldn't choose a cat. He wasn't a cat kind of guy.

For some reason, all he said was "Isn't Rover a dog's name?"

Maggie laughed. "Maybe, but it shouldn't be. Cats rove around a lot more than dogs do." She shrugged. "Of course, now that he's yours, you can call him whatever you want."

Rover finished depositing a scattering of orange cat hair on Neil's khaki slacks and slunk back out of the room. He watched the animal go with a feeling of vague bewilderment. Like it or not, apparently he now owned a cat.

He turned his attention back to Maggie. "Is there something I can help you with?"

"I hope so, but first, let's have a few of these cookies." She waggled the bakery box. "Why don't

I go grab some plates? We'll have a snack and talk for a few minutes before I go back to work."

She headed into the kitchen, leaving Neil behind in the living room. He heard her opening and shutting cupboard doors.

"Where do you keep your dishes?" she called.

This was getting out of hand. No matter how cute this woman was, she still had to respect a man's boundaries. Neil strode to the kitchen doorway.

Maggie was on tiptoe, peeking in a cabinet. It, like most of the cupboards, was completely empty. She glanced at him over one shoulder, raising an eyebrow. "You really *haven't* moved in yet, have you? Or don't you own any plates?"

"I own plates." He opened the deep drawer nearest the stove, and Maggie inspected its contents with frank interest. Two plain white cereal bowls were nested together, two clear glasses were laid side by side, and two matching plates were stacked neatly on top of each other.

"Very efficient." Maggie spoke brightly, but the gentle kindness in her voice made his toes curl.

Plainly, she pitied a man who had only two plates to his name. She'd feel even sorrier for him if she knew that was one plate more than he actually needed.

That hadn't always been the case. He'd donated most of his and Laura's household items when he'd moved, including the huge, mismatched set of dishes they'd used when they'd hosted their frequent backyard barbecues and potluck dinners. He'd kept only what he absolutely needed, and he hadn't needed much.

He'd never considered what his solitary life must look like to other people. Pretty pathetic, he supposed, especially to a woman who threw cheerful friendliness around like confetti.

She set the plates on the small square table, after bumping the drawer closed with her hip. Then she pulled out a chair.

"Well, don't just stand there. Sit."

He stayed where he was, trying to get his bearings. Being around Maggie reminded him of walking into bright sunshine after spending hours hunched over books in the quiet dimness of a library. He felt off-balance and a little blinded.

The woman was unsettling.

"Come on," she coaxed. "I don't bite. And look what I brought!" She lifted the lid on the shiny box. Inside were a half dozen big cookies, each bearing a crisscross design, sparkling with grains of sugar. The aroma drifting out was incredible—rich and peanut buttery. Neil's stomach promptly reminded him he'd forgotten to eat lunch. Again.

Maggie plopped a fat cookie on each plate and frowned. "We're going to need something to drink, and I didn't bring anything. You wouldn't happen to have any milk, would you?"

"Actually, I do," Neil admitted. "I...uh...bought some for the cat."

"That's sweet. But not actually a good idea, you know, giving store-bought milk to a cat."

"So I learned. He drank a great big bowl, then threw up all over the house." He wrinkled his nose, remembering. "It was pretty awful."

"I'd imagine so." Maggie tilted her head, considering him. "Know what you need?"

Whatever it was, it obviously wasn't a cat. He shouldn't have let the animal inside in the first place, much less made a special trip to the grocery store to buy milk for him. He should have handed Rover off to the local vet or the humane society. That would have been the smarter thing to do.

He sighed. "What do I need?"

"Goat's milk."

"Excuse me?"

"Goat's milk is perfectly fine for cats. I'll bring you some, if you want. We have a sweet old nanny over at the farm that we milk every morning. Rover loves her milk, and it won't upset his stomach. In the meantime, why don't you grab whatever milk Rover left for us, and those two glasses, and let's get this party started."

Neil didn't do parties anymore—not even cookies-and-milk parties. But somehow before he knew it, he was splashing a generous slug of milk into their glasses and settling across from Maggie at his tiny table. She picked up her glass and tilted it in his direction.

"To new friends," she toasted cheerfully. "Go ahead. Try your cookie. I baked them myself."

The cookie was as big as the palm of his hand, and when he took a bite, his taste buds went crazy with joy. He hadn't had a cookie like this in…well, ever. It was amazing.

Maggie watched him, her elbows resting on the table, chin in her hands. "Good?"

"Fantastic." He took another big bite.

"I'm glad you like them." She rummaged inside the box and put a second cookie on his plate. "I love to see people enjoying my cooking."

"If they don't enjoy this, there's something wrong with them."

"Aren't you sweet?" Her smile broadened, and he couldn't help it. He smiled back. "Well," she continued, "now that I've got you nicely buttered up, I guess I'd better get to my point. I need to ask you for a favor."

Neil's smile faded. He couldn't imagine any favor he could do for a woman like Maggie. What, exactly, was all this leading up to?

Chapter Three

"What favor?"

Maggie noted the wariness in his expression with a sinking heart. Apparently, the cookies hadn't done as great a job as she'd hoped. "Don't worry. It's nothing big. I just need to ask you a few questions." She tried a smile. "They may seem a little stupid."

"There's no such thing as a stupid question."

"You sound like a teacher," she quipped, hoping for a smile.

She didn't get one. He only arched an eyebrow.

She cleared her throat. Okay, then. No more joking around. "So, exactly what happened this morning between you and Oliver? Can you take me through it step-by-step?"

"Why?" Neil's brow crinkled. "Was he hurt worse than we thought?"

"No," Maggie reassured him. "It's nothing like

that. I just need to figure out how you got through to him."

"What do you mean?"

She shrugged helplessly. She didn't know how else to explain this. "How did you get him to trust you so fast? Did you say anything, do anything special?"

Neil looked genuinely confused. "I didn't 'get through' to Oliver. He screamed. I picked him up and stuck a Band-Aid on his knee. I didn't do anything special."

"Well, something special happened. He's been with me for weeks, and he's never let me carry him like that. It's not for any lack of effort on my part, trust me. I've read dozens of adoption books, and I've tried every strategy they mention. Nothing's worked. Not until today, with you."

"Since you're adopting him, I'm assuming his parents are dead?"

"His mom passed away a little over a month ago. His dad's never been in the picture. The social worker's gone through all the channels to try to locate him without any success, so Oliver's on his own. Or he was. Now he's got Ruby and me."

She saw the question in his eyes before he asked it, but it took him a minute to get it out. "Oliver's mom. What happened to her?"

"Drugs," Maggie answered sadly. "Sierra and I were in the same grade. She didn't come from the greatest family, but she was a nice kid. Really athletic, too. She ran cross-country, and she was good at it. Then she had a pretty serious knee injury at a state match, and she got hooked on her prescription pain pills." Maggie shook her head. "She spiraled down from there. From what we heard, things got pretty rough toward the end." She hesitated, torn between honesty and compassion. "Sierra wasn't able to give Oliver the best care," she finished finally. "He has some trust issues."

"I see," Neil said quietly.

"After Sierra died, Mrs. Darnell from social services called Ruby and asked her to take Oliver as an emergency placement. That's what Ruby does nowadays, short-term fostering until the social workers can figure out where to place a new kid. When I heard about Oliver's situation, I decided to become a licensed parent so that I could foster and hopefully adopt him myself. They agreed to let Oliver stay in Ruby's care until I get through. Then I'll take over legally, and we'll go from there."

"You call your mother by her first name."

Maggie looked up, startled. "I'm sorry?"

"Ruby's your mother, but you always call her by her first name. That's unusual around here."

She shrugged. "Technically, Ruby's my foster mom. I was in the system, just like Oliver, and I came to Sweet Springs Farm when I was twelve. When we met, she told me to call her Ruby, so I did. We all do, but she's our mother, just the same."

"We all?"

"There are six of us kids. Well, six who stayed, three boys and three girls. Others came in and out. I was the first of her HTPs, and I guess since I called her Ruby, the rest of them followed suit. I never thought much about it."

"'HTP'? What does that mean?"

Maggie smiled. "Family shorthand for *hard-to-place*. That was Ruby's specialty. She always asked for the tough cases, the kids nobody else could manage."

"*You* were hard to manage?"

She laughed at the astonishment in his voice. "Is that so hard to believe?"

"Yeah, it is. I don't think you've stopped smiling since I met you."

Maggie laughed again. "The good Lord and Ruby get the credit for that. Now I smile. Before I came to Sweet Springs Farm, not so much. Love has an incredible power to change people for the better."

She saw skepticism in his eyes, but when he spoke, his voice was carefully polite. "I'm glad that's been your experience."

Something was hiding under Neil's statement,

like a pile of trash swept under a rug. Maggie didn't have any idea what it was, but she didn't need to understand to feel sorry for the pain it put in his eyes.

"My brothers and sisters would tell you the same thing," she assured him softly. "That's why I have high hopes that love will eventually reach through to Oliver, as well, even though I haven't seen much progress. Until today, that is. I realize Oliver's reaction to you might not have seemed all that remarkable on your end, but it was a real breakthrough for him." She clasped her hands on top of the table and leaned forward, searching his face. "Are you *sure* there wasn't anything special you did or said? Anything at all that I could copy?"

He shook his head. "I was with him for a half hour, tops. It wasn't long enough for anything meaningful to happen. I'm sorry, but I don't know what else to tell you. Maybe it was just a onetime thing because he was hurt and scared. Maybe it wasn't…*me*. I'm not exactly a little-kid person."

He had a point there. "Maybe you're right. It's a disappointment, though. I hoped today meant things were going to start changing for Oliver."

"I'm sorry."

"Not your fault. Thanks for talking with me." Maggie looked at her watch and winced. "I'm really late. Angelo's going to be beside himself."

When she pushed back her chair and stood, Neil rose to his feet, as well.

"It's a good thing you're doing, Maggie. I wish I could have been more help." He held out his hand. When she accepted it, his fingers closed over hers with such strong warmth that her knees went a little jiggly.

"Thanks."

One corner of his mouth tilted up as he studied her face. "And I'm not just saying that because of the cookies, although they were pretty incredible."

That cute half smile wasn't helping her knee situation any. She gently pulled her hand free and turned toward the front door. "Well, good. I'm glad you like peanut butter. Me, I'm more of a snickerdoodle girl."

"Actually, those are my favorites, too."

"Oh?" Maggie paused, her hand resting on the doorknob. "I make a good snickerdoodle, if I do say so myself. Maybe you can try one on Thursday."

"Thursday?"

"Right." He still looked at her blankly, so she added, "When you come to the bakery for your meeting with Audrey."

Neil muttered a low exclamation and pulled out his phone. He tapped the screen, his expression intent.

"Is something wrong?"

"I'm setting an alarm for that meeting. There." He finished with the phone and returned it to his pocket with a relieved expression. "Now I won't forget. Hopefully."

She watched him with amusement. He looked so serious. "Forget things a lot, do you? Is that why your keys are still hanging from the door-knob?"

"Are they?"

Instead of answering, Maggie opened the front door. The dangling keys jingled.

Neil ran a hand through his hair. "I can't believe I forgot those things *again*."

With that wry embarrassment on his face and his hair standing on end, he looked different. He seemed—approachable. Friendly, even. "At least it fits, you being a history teacher and all. The absentminded-professor bit, I mean."

The warmth in his eyes chilled so fast that Maggie sucked in a sharp breath. What on earth had she said?

He reached past her and pulled the keys out of the doorknob, dropping them into his pocket. "You'd better get to work. Goodbye, Maggie. I hope everything works out with Oliver."

"Bye." Before she finished the syllable, he'd shut the door.

Maggie stood on the sun-warmed porch, biting her lip. The old Sawyer homesite had settled into a harmony with its surroundings long years ago. Songbirds warbled cheerfully in the oaks and pines surrounding the cabin, and a gentle summer breeze ruffled the hairs on the back of her neck. Mingled odors of hot pine needles and sweet summer roses drifted through the air.

This was a calm and peaceful place, but right now Maggie felt anything but calm and peaceful.

She felt like she should knock on the door and apologize. The problem was, she wasn't sure what to apologize for. So, after a few uncomfortable seconds, she went slowly down the steps.

She really did have to get to work. Besides, whatever pain Neil was carrying around, it wasn't any of Maggie's business. It wasn't as if she could do anything to help him.

Although, there was one very small thing she could do. On Thursday morning, she could bake a nice big batch of snickerdoodles.

"You want me to do *what*?"

That Thursday afternoon, Neil leaned over the dainty table, his focus on the trim, middle-aged woman sitting across from him. The bread-scented bakery buzzed busily around them, and he hoped he hadn't heard his principal correctly.

"Consider taking fall semester off," Audrey Aniston repeated clearly.

Before he could respond, Maggie paused by the

table, a carafe of coffee in one hand. "So? What do you think of the coconut cake?" She topped off their cups.

The older woman smiled up at her. "I like it even better than the chocolate, which I honestly didn't think was possible. You're making this decision awfully hard, Maggie."

"That's what I like to hear!" Maggie included Neil in her warm smile, but he didn't smile back. His brain was still trying to wrap itself around what Audrey had just said.

Take another whole semester off after being bumped from summer school? He couldn't handle so many empty days in a row.

That wasn't speculation. It was a stone-cold fact.

"I have one more sample for you," Maggie was saying. "And fair warning. I've saved the best for last." Maggie nimbly gathered their small plates with her free hand and headed toward the kitchen.

He waited until she was out of earshot before speaking. "When I took this job two years ago, it was with the understanding that I'd always be on the summer school roster. Now, not only have you cut me from that schedule, but you're benching me for half the school year?"

Audrey's smile dimmed. "I'm not *benching* you, as you put it. I'm suggesting you consider using some of your accumulated sick leave to take a short break from teaching."

That sure sounded like benching to him. "Why?"

The older woman rested her elbows on the table, her eyes intent on his. "You really want to know? Fine. Here it is. According to your former principal, before your wife's death, you were an extraordinary educator. You had a reputation as a teacher who could reach any student, and I know for a fact that you've won more awards than the rest of my faculty put together. I needed to rejuvenate the history department, and you sounded like just the man to do it, so I jumped on the chance to snag you. But in the two years you've been here, I haven't seen that Neil Hamilton. You come in and teach your classes, but you're—disengaged. Your failure rates are through the roof, and I'm getting complaints. When I've come to observe, it's clear that you're not connecting with your students at all. Do you know what the kids call you? *Iceman*." She leaned back in her chair, waiting for his reaction.

Neil didn't answer. He'd known about the nickname. He just hadn't cared.

He hadn't cared much about anything, not for a long time. He'd focused on getting through each day as it came, and that had been hard enough.

"Look, Neil," Audrey said. "I'm not ready to

give up on you. You're a one-in-a-million educator—or you used to be. You're a rare bird, and
the school needs you." She paused, then went on
more gently. "From what I hear, after your wife's
death, you powered through, barely missing any
work. You haven't taken a single sick day since
you've been here, either. I think you're emotion-
ally burned out, and the best cure for that is to
step away for a while. Take up a hobby, maybe
even look into some grief counseling. I can get
you a few names, if you're interested."

He wasn't. He wasn't talking about his personal
life with some stranger. He jerked off his glasses
and massaged his forehead. "I'm not taking a semester off. I have to work, Audrey."

"Well, something's got to change if you want
to keep your job. I have to consider what's best
for the school. I need the old Neil back, the man
whose stellar résumé is on file in my office. He's
the teacher I hired, and he's the one I expect to
see in your classroom."

Then they had a problem. Because Neil wasn't
sure that guy existed anymore.

"Ta-da!" Maggie swooped in and slid plates
with dainty cake slices in front of each of them.
"Pecan Praline Cake! My personal creation, and
it's fabulous, if I do say so myself. Angelo's eaten
four pieces already this morning."

"Two pieces, I ate," the bald, mustached owner bellowed from the back. "The girl exaggerates!"

"It was four," Maggie whispered with a wink. "Angelo just doesn't like to admit anybody else can come up with a good recipe. You'll never believe this is sugar-free, Audrey."

The principal forked up a generous bite of cake topped with nut-studded icing. The minute it was in her mouth, she moaned. "Oh, my! This is definitely the one. I'm officially placing an order. My sister's going to love this. Taste it, Neil. It's amazing. Maggie here has a real gift."

"I know," he replied absently, his mind still focused on those three awful words. *A semester off.* "She brought cookies to my house."

"Did she?" His principal glanced between him and Maggie with an arched eyebrow. "That's—interesting."

"Oh, he earned them, fair and square," Maggie said cheerfully. "Audrey, remember how I was telling you about Oliver, the little boy I'm planning to adopt? Ruby and I've been struggling to reach him, but Neil connected with him right off. It's the first encouraging sign we've seen."

Maggie rested a hand on his shoulder as she spoke. He startled, then went still, as if a butterfly had fluttered down to light on him. The warmth of her fingers seeped through the crisp cotton of his shirt. It had been a long while since a woman had touched him, he realized suddenly.

"Maggie," a gray-haired woman in a pink pant-suit called from a neighboring table. "Could we get some refills, please?"

"Coming, Edna!" Maggie gave his shoulder a squeeze, then whisked to the counter to collect the coffeepot. Neil's gaze trailed her as she bustled around the little bakery. She hovered over the elderly customers as if they were the most important people on earth.

Apparently, baking wasn't the only gift Maggie had. She also had a knack for making people feel as if they were something special—even when they really weren't.

He'd best remember that.

Audrey was studying him with an odd expression. "You connected with a child Ruby Sawyer couldn't reach? That's impressive."

From the tone of the principal's voice, *impressive* was polite code for *unbelievable.*

"Maggie's reading too much into it. All I did was put a Band-Aid on the kid's knee. I don't know why he liked me."

"But he did. That's an encouraging sign, Neil. For both of you, maybe." She paused, then added, "You know, after my husband died, my pastor suggested that I do some volunteering at the church. It was hard at first, getting out, interacting with people, but it did me a lot of good. Maggie," Audrey called as Maggie swooped by the table, "are you still looking for help with the summer lunch program on Wednesday mornings?"

"Are you kidding? Between the school lunches and all the other events we're catering, my summer schedule's jam-packed. I'll take all the help I can get. Are you offering?"

"Actually, I was thinking about Neil here. He's at loose ends this summer and looking for something meaningful to do."

"Oh!" Maggie's and Neil's eyes locked. For a second, she looked just as blindsided as he felt, but then she smiled. "If he's got the time, that would be wonderful!"

Neil wasn't sure *wonderful* was the right word. He had no idea what they were talking about. "What's the summer lunch program?"

Before Audrey could answer, Maggie jumped in. "It's a wonderful outreach. A huge percentage of our students here in Cedar Ridge qualify for free lunches, and for a lot of kids, that's the only decent meal they get for the whole day. Audrey was concerned that they'd go hungry during the summer, so she started this program. The restaurants in town take turns donating bagged lunches every weekday, and we pass them out in the parking lot of the high school." She smiled warmly at Audrey. "It's a brilliant idea."

"It's an expensive idea," Angelo grouched from the kitchen doorway. "I shoulda never let you talk me into it."

"Oh, hush," Maggie called back affectionately. "Angelo's not nearly as hard-hearted as he'd like people to think. He's buying fresh fruit for the kids out of his own pocket."

"Stop telling people my business," the old man bellowed.

Maggie blew a sassy raspberry in his direction, and Angelo made a face at her before disappearing into the kitchen.

Maggie turned her attention back to Neil. "I've got three hundred sandwiches to make next Wednesday morning, so I'd love some help. I start early, though. Six a.m. That's a deal breaker for most folks."

"Maggie, could we get our check?" one of the elderly ladies called. "We need to get to our book club meeting."

"Coming," Maggie responded, pulling her order pad out of her apron pocket.

Neil watched her go. Did the woman ever sit down? She seemed to have an inexhaustible energy.

"Neil?" His principal was looking at him earnestly. "Volunteering with Maggie could do you a world of good. If that girl can't show you how to connect with people, nobody can. Plus, you'll be interacting with a lot of your own students outside of the classroom. That might help you develop some rapport with them." Audrey tilted her head. "What do you say?"

There was only one answer to that question, and it wasn't just because he wanted back in Audrey's good graces. Maybe he wasn't the teacher he'd once been, but if his students were going hungry right under his nose, he wouldn't sit on his hands and do nothing.

He wasn't that far gone. Not quite.

"Sure, I'll help."

"Great!" Audrey smiled. "We'll thaw the Iceman yet." She scraped up the last bite of cake and rose. "I'll be praying for you, Neil. I want you on my staff, but make no mistake. If I don't see some difference in you over the course of the next school year, more enthusiasm, more connection with the kids…well." She shook her head. "Let's just say I'll be facing a really tough decision."

She was out the door before he could respond.

So that was that. Neil eyed the untasted cake sample on his plate. His conversation with Audrey had killed his appetite.

At some level, he'd known he was just going through the motions at school. When a swimmer was trying not to drown, he focused on getting air into his lungs one breath at a time. He didn't worry much about whether his form was winning points with the judges.

But he hadn't fully realized how low he'd sunk professionally until today. In the old days, he'd have been the one spearheading the summer lunch program, and now he hadn't even noticed the problem until somebody else pointed it out.

He felt sick.

After Laura's death, he'd clung doggedly to his profession, hoping eventually his passion for teaching would come back. In the meantime, at least the work filled up his dark, empty days. He'd known he wasn't the teacher he'd once been, but he'd at least figured himself to be competent.

Obviously not.

Audrey was right. It was time to make a decision. Staying in the classroom wasn't an option, not if this was the best he could do. If he'd lost his gift for teaching, he'd have to find another job. One that didn't involve working with students.

A wave of sad weariness washed over him at the thought.

He'd always wanted to teach. Always. Now he was losing that on top of everything else.

"You're going to hurt my feelings."

Maggie stood beside him, holding a bakery box in her hands. She nodded toward his untouched cake.

"Oh." He scooped up a mouthful.

He'd only meant to be polite, but there was something comforting about the rich sweetness. When he finished that bite, he forked up another one. Maggie cocked her head to one side, watching him. A smile tickled around her mouth, making her dimples play hide-and-seek in her cheeks.

"Good?" she asked him.

"*Really* good," he answered honestly. "Best cake I've ever tasted."

"Thanks." The tickle of a smile turned into a broad one. "Just for that, your coffee's on the house today."

"Nobody gets free coffee." Glowering, Angelo poked his head through the kitchen doorway.

"Take it out of my tips," Maggie called without turning around.

"I'll pay for it." Neil set down his fork, intending to reach for his wallet, but Maggie shook her head.

"No, please. The coffee's on me. And so are these." She set the box on the table. "Snickerdoodles."

His favorite cookies. He'd forgotten he'd told her that. "You didn't have to—"

She nudged the box in his direction. "I know I didn't have to, silly. I wanted to."

"Well. Thanks." He hesitated, but curiosity won out. "How are things going with Oliver? Have you seen any improvement?"

The sparkle in Maggie's eyes dimmed. "Not really. After the way he acted with you the other day, I'd hoped to see some changes, but so far, nothing."

That was pretty much what he'd expected to hear, but he found himself wishing things had turned out differently for her. "I'm sorry."

"Oh, I'm not giving up. Sooner or later, I'll figure out how to reach him."

She sounded as if she were trying to convince herself, and Neil searched his mind for something encouraging to say. Before he came up with anything, the bell suspended above the bakery door jingled.

Ruby walked in, ushering Oliver ahead of her. The little boy had a stony expression on his face, and he was doing his best to stay out of reach. Ruby looked tired, but she smiled and waved when she caught Neil's eye.

"Look who's here!" Maggie's face lit up. "Hi, Ruby. Hello, sweetie. What perfect timing. I just took a fresh batch of chocolate chip cookies out of the oven, and—"

Oliver glanced up sullenly, his expression shuttered. Then his eyes widened and a huge smile spread across his face.

Pulling away from Ruby, the toddler darted across the bakery, weaving through the scattered tables. Maggie dropped to her knees on the tiled floor, holding her arms out wide as Oliver made a beeline in her direction.

At the last minute, he veered to the left, skirting Maggie's expectant arms and heading straight for Neil. Oliver halted in front of Neil's chair, lifted his chubby hands and flexed his fingers urgently, his eyes pleading.

Neil heard Maggie's sharp intake of breath and Ruby's worried murmur from the doorway. "Oh, my."

Neil looked uncertainly from Maggie to the little face peering hopefully up into his own. She gave him a quick nod as she rose slowly to her feet. *Go ahead.*

"Hi, Oliver. How are you doing, buddy?" Neil picked the toddler up under his armpits and settled the child on his lap. To him, the whole thing felt painfully awkward, but Oliver didn't seem to agree. Sighing deeply, the tiny boy stuck his thumb in his mouth and laid his head contentedly against Neil's chest.

Maggie looked down at them with a yearning expression, her face pale and her eyes shimmering with unshed tears.

"I'm sorry," Neil said. "I don't know why—"

"Please don't apologize." Scrubbing briskly at her eyes with the back of her hand, Maggie managed a wobbly smile. "It's good," she assured him in a whisper. "I wish it was me. But it's good that it's somebody, right? Thanks for being so nice to him. I really appreciate… Excuse me just a minute, okay?"

She turned away and hurried toward the kitchen. Angelo, his florid face somber and worried, stepped silently away from the doorway to let her pass and then closed the door gently behind her.

As Neil watched her go, his heart twisted hard inside his chest, and a longing rose up with so much power that he felt stunned.

For the first time in over three years, he desperately wanted to help another human being.

The problem was, he had no idea how.

Chapter Four

Early the following Wednesday morning, Maggie stood Oliver on a sturdy chair pulled up to the bakery's stainless-steel work counter. The little boy stiffened and moved to the far edge of the chair's seat. She took a step back, staying within arms' reach but allowing him as much space as she could.

"Okay, sweetie!" she said brightly. "Ready to help me make some lunches?"

Oliver's only response was to kneel and clamber off the chair. Maggie stifled a sigh. Well, it had been worth a try.

Oliver had woken up this morning as she'd been getting ready to come to the bakery, and she hadn't liked the idea of leaving him behind. Ruby needed her sleep, and Maggie didn't trust him not to slip off again.

Besides, working together was a good way to

encourage bonding. Over the years, Maggie had seen Ruby use this tactic many times to get her kids to open up. In fact, she still pulled that particular stunt on occasion—and it usually worked. That was one reason Maggie was thrilled that Angelo had no problem with her bringing Oliver along to the bakery.

Unfortunately, so far she was still batting zero. She kept one eye on the toddler as she went to the cooler to get the large tub of chicken salad she'd made the day before. What she saw wasn't encouraging. He'd backed as far away from Maggie as he could get. He was sucking his thumb, eyes downcast, his expression blank.

Her heart clenched. She knew that closed-off look. She'd felt it on her own face many times growing up, and she hated to think what would've happened if Ruby hadn't broken through the self-protective walls Maggie had built.

Please, Lord, help Oliver to trust me. Help me find a way to—

A firm knock interrupted her silent prayer. "Maggie?" a male voice called from outside the latched back door. "Are you in there?"

Neil had arrived, and according to the big clock ticking on the wall, he was right on time. Six o'clock on the dot.

She smiled. He must have been able to find his keys today.

"Coming!" As she spoke, Oliver launched out of his corner, running toward the door. In a red-hot second, he was pulling frantically on the doorknob.

Maggie's heart cracked a little more. The other day, when Oliver had bypassed her hug and thrown himself at Neil, she'd tried to focus on the blessing in it. She really had.

But it hadn't been easy.

For one beautiful split second, she'd thought Oliver was running to *her*, that all her dreams and hopes were coming true. That instant of pure joy had only made the disappointment sharper.

"Just a minute, sweetie. I have to unlock it." She disengaged the lock, gently shepherding Oliver backward so she could open the door. He shied away from her touch like always, but the minute the crack was wide enough, he wedged through.

The little boy threw himself at the man standing on the top step, wrapping his arms tightly around Neil's knees. Thrown off balance, he grabbed for the doorjamb to steady himself and looked at Maggie, his expression bewildered.

She forced a smile. "Somebody's glad to see you."

Neil looked down at the child pressed against his khakis. "Hold this." He passed Maggie a stainless-steel travel mug that smelled of coffee. Gently, Neil disentangled Oliver's hands and knelt on the steps, looking into the toddler's face.

"Hiya, kiddo. Are you going to be helping us today?"

The little boy nodded rapidly, and Neil smiled.

"Good! Sounds like we've got a lot of lunches to make, so I guess we'd better get to work, huh?" Neil scooped Oliver up, and the little boy relaxed against the man's chest.

In spite of her best intentions, jealousy pricked her heart. She'd give anything for Oliver to nestle in her arms like that.

Maggie knew life rarely played fair. She'd cut her teeth on that unpleasant nugget of truth. Still, it seemed wrong for a virtual stranger to get this reaction, when she'd tried so hard and gotten nowhere.

She'd talked out her frustration with Ruby the other night over mugs of cocoa in the farmhouse kitchen.

What's he doing that I'm not? Maggie had asked despairingly. *Oliver barely knows him, and you have to admit Neil Hamilton isn't a warm and fuzzy kind of guy.*

Oh, honey, who knows? Ruby had shaken her head. *Maybe Neil don't come across as the friendliest fellow, but something about him sure speaks to our Oliver. We just got to figure out what it is.*

"Maggie?"

"Hmm?" She glanced up to find Neil studying her.

"Hadn't we better get started?"

"Oh." Maggie blinked. "Yes, we should. Come on in, and I'll show you the ropes." She waved toward the bakery's spotless food-prep area.

Neil paused to close the door, juggling Oliver clumsily in his arms. "Do I need to lock this again?"

"No, that's all right. Angelo grew up in a rough neighborhood, and he worries, the softhearted goof. He makes me lock it when I'm here by myself. But now that you're here, it's fine." Neil gave off a brainy vibe, but he also had a set of don't-mess-with-me shoulders going on. Even Angelo wouldn't worry about her safety with Neil around.

She went to the counter, motioning for Neil to follow. He did, and when he noticed the chair she'd pulled up, he set Oliver on it. Maggie's stomach twinged when the boy scooted to the edge again, this time to press closer to Neil's side.

Neil was frowning. "What's he like to work for?"

"Angelo? He's a great boss. Here." She set his coffee mug in front of him, then slid over the tub of chicken salad. "You fill the sandwiches. They're the heaviest thing in the lunch, so they'll go in the bottom of the bag."

"He seems to yell at you a lot."

Maggie went to retrieve the first of three large plastic containers full of croissants. "Oh, he doesn't mean anything by it. It's like how he fusses about donating food to all these summer outreaches. He's really the most generous man alive. He gave me my first job back when I was fifteen, and he's always paid me over scale. And he's been a gem about letting me bring Oliver along to work, too. Angelo blusters, but deep down, he's a big old ball of mush." She snapped off the lid, and the comforting odor of buttery bread wafted upward, making her heart do a tiny leap of happiness.

She did appreciate good food.

"You're using croissants?" Neil sounded incredulous.

"Today we are. Last time we had pita bread stuffed with shaved ham and mozzarella." She handed him a box of plastic gloves. "I'll slice the croissants, and you can fill them and stick them in the baggies. Then we put them in the lunch sack. We'll add pretzels, then a cookie and a napkin, and we'll store the bags in the coolers." She nodded toward the insulated containers lined against the wall as she picked up a serrated knife. "There's no separate fruit today because Angelo insisted on adding plenty of grapes and pecans to the salad. 'Those kids'll eat more fruit if you mix it with the good stuff.'" She mimicked

Angelo's gruff growl. "He's right, too," she admitted. "Of course, adding those ingredients made the chicken salad three times as expensive. Like I told you, big ball of mush."

She passed him a sliced croissant and watched as he glopped the chunky salad over the bread. "We won't add mayo because it's already in the salad, and we don't want them getting soggy. No, put a little more. That's it. There's a sweet spot between not enough and so much that the sandwich explodes." She nodded as he awkwardly stuffed the filled croissant into a flimsy baggie. "There you go. Now, just do that two hundred and ninety-nine more times."

She was rewarded with a wry smile as he tackled the next croissant. "Messy job," he observed. "Wouldn't something like ham and cheese be easier?"

Maggie felt a twinge of irritation, but she squashed it good-naturedly. He didn't understand. Most people didn't. "Easier, sure. Better, nope."

She deftly sliced the rolls, stacking them on the stainless-steel counter at Neil's elbow. She'd better hurry and get these done so she could help with the rest of the prep work. They'd never get finished in time at this rate.

She watched him out of the corner of her eye as they worked. Like most people unused to food service, Neil started off slow, but he got a little faster as they went, still careful to put exactly the right amount of chicken salad on each croissant half. She felt herself relaxing as they found their rhythm.

"You do this every week?" Neil put another finished sandwich into a brown bag and added it to the growing line on the counter.

"Just about, until school starts back up." She put down the knife. She'd give him a chance to play catch-up while she moved their finished sandwiches temporarily into the walk-in fridge. She didn't want them sitting at room temperature too long. She grabbed a tray and began to line it with the opened bags.

"This is a lot of work for you."

Maggie laughed. "I guess it is, but I don't mind. Kitchens are my happy places. The heart of the home, and all that." She glanced affectionately around the bakery. "I think of Angelo's kitchen as the heart of Cedar Ridge. I love working here."

As she reached for the farthest bag, she leaned near Oliver. The little boy shrank away, pressing himself closer to Neil's side. Maggie winced, but she made herself smile.

"Excuse me, Oliver," she murmured.

Sympathy flickered in Neil's eyes. "Your mom's a really nice lady," he said. Oliver looked up adoringly when Neil spoke, and when he mentioned Maggie, the child looked over at her. To her astonishment, the wary little boy's eyes connected directly with hers, making her breath catch in her throat. She swallowed and smiled encouragingly.

Oliver didn't smile back, but he held her gaze for a precious second or two. Then he looked away, stuck his thumb back in his mouth and leaned his head against Neil's side.

Maggie's heart soared. Eye contact was huge. All the attachment experts said so, and she'd struggled from the start to get any from the little boy. This, she told herself firmly, was real progress. A tiny step forward, maybe, but a real one.

She smiled at Neil. *Thank you*, she mouthed silently. Like Oliver, he didn't smile back, but the eyes behind the glasses crinkled at the corners, and he nodded.

They worked companionably after that. When the sandwiches were finally finished, Maggie flexed her cramped fingers. "We're in the home stretch. Now we put in the pretzels and the cookies and a napkin." She retrieved the cookie containers and lined the elements up on the counter. "Then we fold the tops and put the bags in the coolers to transport to the school." She popped the top off the first cookie tub, and as Neil leaned over to look, she felt a thrill of happy anticipation.

She'd been trying to think of a good cookie idea all week. She'd been stumped until last Saturday. The temp had topped eighty-five, and she'd pulled last year's flip-flops from the back of her closet. That was when it had struck her—the perfect summer-vacation cookie.

After a quick study of Pinterest, she'd baked them. Three hundred sugar-cookie flip-flops, iced with various colorful designs and enclosed in cellophane bags tied with curly blue and green ribbons. Maggie surveyed them proudly, breathing in their comforting aroma. They'd turned out well, even if she did say so herself.

"What do you think?"

"Those?" He glanced at her, his eyebrows raised. "We're putting *those* in brown paper bags?"

"Sure. Aren't they cute?"

"They're…elaborate. They must have taken you hours." He lifted a cookie, iced green with sunny yellow straps and polka dots.

"Well, yeah, but they were fun. They taste good, too. Here." She pulled a broken cookie from her scrap tin. "I always save the casualties for taste-testing."

He snapped the cookie piece in two and handed half to Oliver, who accepted it happily. Once again, Maggie felt a jab of envy. When she'd begged Oliver to taste these cookies, all she'd gotten was a cold look.

She sighed and turned her attention back to Neil. "So?"

"They're great."

There was a strange tone in his voice. "What's wrong?"

"Nothing. It's just…" He gestured at the clutter surrounding them. "Croissants, homemade chicken salad, these fancy cookies. This isn't what I expect when I think of a kid's sack lunch."

"Obviously you haven't been eating *my* lunches," Maggie informed him with a laugh.

"This doesn't seem like overkill to you? I lived on PB&J sandwiches when I was a kid, and if I dropped one, I just shook the dirt off and ate it anyway. Do you really think they're going to appreciate all the extra work you put into this?"

Overkill. She froze in the act of putting one of the cookies in a bag. "Probably not," she agreed quietly. "But just because they don't know to appreciate my best efforts doesn't mean they don't deserve them. I'll deal with the cookies. Can you manage the rest?"

There was a beat of silence before he answered. "Sure. I'll do the pretzels, and Oliver can be in charge of the napkins."

"I don't think he feels like—" Maggie broke off as Oliver obediently stuffed a flip-flop-printed napkin into the sack Neil slid toward him.

"Good job!" Neil chucked a bag of pretzels in another sack and pushed it toward the toddler. "Next."

Oliver grinned and put in another napkin.

Neil grinned back. "We make a good team, buddy."

Maggie's smile wobbled as she returned her attention to putting the colorful cookies into each bag.

Yes, Neil and Oliver made a wonderful team. Too bad her name still wasn't on the roster.

Neil was assigned the job of carting the heavy coolers from the bakery van to the tables they'd set up in front of Cedar Ridge High School. Since Oliver insisted on clutching a fistful of Neil's pant leg and walking alongside, it was slow going. When he finally lugged up the last ice chest, Maggie was struggling with a disposable tablecloth.

The sea-blue plastic rectangle billowed in the breeze blowing off the mountains, and Maggie's lips pursed in a pout of concentration as she battled it down. She made a colorful picture against the blue, with her spring-green shirt and her red curls shimmering in the sun. As he watched, a gust of wind whipped the edge of the tablecloth out of her grip, and she laughed out loud as she fought to reclaim it.

The joy in that unselfconscious laugh hit Neil like a blow. When was the last time he'd laughed like that? He couldn't remember. And yet in spite of her worries about Oliver, Maggie was still able to enjoy herself.

"There!" She clamped the last corner of the material onto the table with a triumphant grin. "Now, behave yourself." She bent to rummage in a striped tote and produced several pairs of brand-new flip-flops in various colors and patterns. She scattered them along the edge of the table.

He frowned. "What are you doing?"

"Decorating."

Decorating. With shoes. Okay. "Need any help?"

"Thanks, but I've got it." She straightened and shaded her eyes. Knots of kids and teenagers were ambling down the sidewalk, and cars were pulling into the parking lot. "Just in time, too. You man the drinks, and I'll pass out the lunches."

"Sure. Do we have some kind of list to go by?"

"Nope." Maggie began pulling lunches out of one of the coolers. "Put the ice chest on the table and pop the top. The kids like to pick their own drinks, and the line moves faster that way."

Neil heaved the cooler onto the table and lifted the lid, revealing layers of juice boxes and milk cartons nestled in ice. "If you don't have a list, how do you know who's supposed to get the food?"

Maggie laughed. "Simple. If they're hungry, they get a lunch. Hi!" She waved to a group of approaching girls. "How are y'all doing?"

Kids flocked to the table, accepting the lunches and the hugs Maggie offered with equal enthusiasm. Their careless chatter slowed when they reached Neil. The kids, many of them his own students, slanted him a cautious glance before pawing quickly through the ice to make their drink choice.

None of them seemed inclined to make conversation—much less to hug him—so there was nothing much for him to do except observe the kids' reactions to their fancy lunches. So he did.

The sandwiches were well received, and most of the kids had a mouthful of chicken salad before they'd walked three feet away from the tables. But Maggie's flip-flop cookies were the real hit of the day.

The girls squealed, trading among themselves to get a cookie that better matched their outfits. Even the guys seemed impressed—although, Neil noticed they actually ate their cookies, while the girls stowed theirs carefully in purses.

"Well, ain't this something? Iceman's manning the ice." Dex Greene, one of his American history students, was rummaging through the drinks. "What happened, man? You being punished for something?"

"Nope, just helping out." Neil spoke evenly. He and Dex had tangled repeatedly last year over the teen's habit of skipping class. When the kid had blown off the final exam, he'd flunked him. Dex requested a meeting so he could "explain" and get another shot at taking the test, but Neil had made it clear that the fail was final. They hadn't parted on the best of terms.

"Yeah, that sounds like you. Real helpful." Dex snorted a skeptical laugh. "You got any apple juice left?"

"I think there's some at the bottom." A disturbing number of his students had turned up today. Would they have gone hungry without this outreach? He'd had no idea so many of their families were struggling financially. How had he missed that?

Also disturbing was the fact that Dex was the only one who'd spoken to him. On the other hand, almost every kid coming through the line had not only spoken to Maggie but hugged her, as well. They all seemed to know her, and she remembered more of their names than he did.

This wasn't good. He'd been more disconnected than he'd realized.

Dex rummaged in the ice until he unearthed a small green box with an apple on the front. "Awesome!" The boy leaned down, and for the first time, Neil noticed a tiny child clinging to Dex's left hand.

Dex caught him looking. "I know he's not a student, but Maggie said it was all right," the teenager said defensively. "Rory can't have milk. He's allergic. But he's okay with apple juice."

Neil nodded. "No problem. Help yourself."

"Dex," Maggie called from the other end of the table. "You forgot your other bag."

The boy shot Neil a wary look. "That's okay, Mags. Rory and I can share. I know it's one lunch per customer."

"That rule doesn't apply to you, kiddo. Here." Maggie tossed a bag in Dex's direction. He caught it handily and grinned.

"You got a good arm, Mags."

That was right, Neil remembered. Dex played baseball. Or he had. Now that he'd failed history, he wouldn't be eligible.

Dex looked back at Neil. "That's Maggie's kid, isn't it?" He nodded at Oliver. The toddler was standing close to Neil, sucking his thumb.

"Yes." He laid a hand on Oliver's head. "He's a friend of mine. Better grab another drink for yourself, Dex. Not enough in that little box for two people."

His former student lifted an eyebrow as he reached back into the cooler for a carton of milk. "Careful there, Iceman. Somebody might get the idea that you actually got a heart." The teen offered Neil a mock salute, then led his toddling charge into the shade of an oak. The two of them settled in the grass to explore their lunches.

The line had thinned, but most of the kids hung around, eating their lunches picnic-style on the ground. Maggie was busily setting the remaining few lunches out on her table. She glanced up as Neil walked over.

"That was nice of you," he said, "letting Dex have an extra lunch for his brother."

Maggie's eyes strayed to Dex, who was carefully breaking up the pretzels for Rory and laying them on a napkin unfolded on the ground. "You know Dex?"

"He was in my American history class last year. Occasionally. When he wasn't cutting school."

"Ah." Maggie set another lunch on the table. "Well, I'm not surprised he missed class. Last year was tough for them. Their mom passed away in October."

"What?" Neil frowned. He hadn't known that. "I've been a little…out of touch lately. What happened?"

"Car accident." Maggie wiped her hands on her apron. "She was from the next town over, so I didn't know her well, but it was really tragic. The dad's not in the picture, so Rory and Dex moved in with their grandmother. She's not in the best of health, and it took the doctors a while to get Rory's milk allergy diagnosed, so he's been sick a lot, too. Dex has had his hands full. Hey!" She raised her voice and waved at the students.

"Do me a favor and come get the extra lunches and drinks, okay? I don't want to lug this stuff back to the bakery. And if anybody wants these flip-flops, take them, too." There was a rush to the tables, and in no time all the remaining food was claimed.

All the flip-flops vanished, too, except for one suspiciously small red, white and blue pair. Maggie wiggled them in Dex's direction.

"Would these fit Rory?"

The boy loped over and took the shoes from her hand, turning them over to check the size. "Yeah! Thanks, Mags."

"Phooey. Thank *you* for not making me pack them up and take them home," she answered cheerily. She turned to Neil. "Do you mind helping me load up the coolers? Just dump out the ice here and put them in the van for me. Then you're all done."

She spoke politely, but there was a reserve in her voice that hadn't been there before. Clearly, he'd slipped a few notches in Maggie Byrne's opinion.

He didn't blame her. He was Dex Greene's teacher, for crying out loud. How had he not known that Dex had lost his only parent in a car accident?

If anybody could empathize with that loss, Neil certainly could, but he hadn't even known about it, though he was sure the tragedy must have been talked about at school. He'd have heard about it, if he'd been listening.

He hadn't been. If he had, he'd have found out that fully half of his students needed help to get a square meal during summer vacation.

Well, Audrey was right. He'd disengaged with a vengeance. No wonder she'd wanted to bench him.

He poured out the melting ice and carried the coolers to the bakery van, a process once again made more complicated by Oliver. Apparently sensing that Neil was gearing up to leave, the little boy glommed on like glue.

He didn't mind. Maybe having a kid stuck to you like a burr made the job tougher, but it felt better than getting the cold shoulder from kids you'd seen every weekday for nine months.

And deserving it.

When everything was finally loaded, he latched the van's back doors. Maggie slipped her deflated tote bag over one shoulder. She'd clapped a floppy straw hat on her head, and its open weave threw shadow sprinkles over her face. Even standing in a ninety-degree parking lot with a sheen of sweat on her face, the woman managed to look cute.

"Thanks, Neil," she said politely. "You were a big help."

He hadn't been, not really, but he was glad he'd

come. It had been an eye-opening experience. "You're welcome."

"We'd better go. I need to run Oliver back to Ruby's and then get to the bakery. Angelo's already handled the lunch rush by himself, and he's probably ready to go hide in the kitchen for the rest of the afternoon."

Suddenly, Neil felt reluctant to end things this way, with this new coolness between them.

"You were right," he blurted out. "About the fancy lunches, I mean. The kids loved them."

She tilted her head. The shadow spots danced merrily over her cheeks like extra freckles, but her face was uncharacteristically serious. "Folks like to be fussed over. Especially these kids, because they don't get enough of that kind of attention." She smiled, and the shift in her expression did something funny to the pit of his stomach. "I can see why it might've seemed silly. But when a person turns to me for help, I think they deserve the best I can give them. Today my best just happened to be flip-flop cookies and chicken salad croissants, that's all. Come on, sweetie." She reached for Oliver. "Let's go see Grandma Ruby."

Shaking his head furiously, the toddler gripped Neil's shirt and set up a howl that echoed against the brick walls of the school. He struggled and kicked as Maggie tried to disentangle him. Neil winced as Oliver pummeled her with his feet.

"Do you want me to buckle him into the car seat for you?"

"That's okay." Maggie's hat was askew, and her face looked ashen as she spoke over Oliver's cries. "I'll manage. Ruby and I will get him settled down once I take him home. Thanks again, Neil."

The child's protesting screams turned into sobs when Maggie finally succeeded in pulling him into her arms. He sagged limply in her embrace, crying pitifully as she buckled him into the car seat.

Neil waited until the bakery van had bumped out of the parking lot, until he could no longer hear Oliver's now-muffled howls. He gave the high school building a long look before heading for his Jeep.

He'd better get back to the cabin and settle in. He had some serious thinking to do.

Chapter Five

Neil tapped his computer keys and clicked Send. Then he stretched and glanced at the clock on the fireplace mantel.

It was almost two o'clock in the morning, and he was midway through one of his sleepless bouts. That was nothing unusual.

Since Laura died, he'd spent plenty of nights pacing the house and watching the clock. Over the past few years, his insomnia had shifted from chronic to sporadic. He'd sleep all right for a few nights, maybe even a week. Then it would come back in full force. There usually was no particular rhyme or reason to it, but this time, he knew exactly what had triggered it.

It had been a long time since he'd interacted with his students outside the classroom, three years since he'd looked at the kids and seen them as more than just names on a roster. Back when he'd been in his sweet spot as a teacher, that had been different.

Once upon a time, he'd gone to every sporting event, known about every triumph and failure, kept a weather eye on moods and relationships as well as grades and averages. He'd headed up after-school clubs and volunteered for field trips and extra bus duty.

He'd taught his classes dressed in period costume at least three times a year. He'd helped students build a working catapult, and once, when every single one of his students had passed their midterm exams, he'd made good on a rash promise and ridden a borrowed horse into the lunchroom in full medieval armor.

That stunt had gotten him a half-hearted reprimand from the principal. It had also scored him a full-page spread in the yearbook, a page he'd signed for the over two hundred students who'd crowded around him when the books were distributed. Those kids hadn't called him Iceman. They'd called him Prof, and they'd had his personal phone number, his ear and a big chunk of his heart.

For Prof, teaching had been more than a job. It had been a mission. A passion.

A joy.

Back then, not only would he have known about his students going hungry in the summertime, he'd have done something about it. No kid went without anything he or she needed, not on his watch. And he definitely would have known about Dex's situation. Prof had always been the first to know things like that.

Right up until the day one of his students had decided to answer a text while driving to school. He'd T-boned Laura as she turned into the faculty parking lot to bring her absentminded husband the wallet he'd forgotten on the bedside table. Again.

Laura and their soon-to-be-born son hadn't been the only ones who'd died that day. Prof had died, too. Neil just hadn't fully realized it until tonight.

That was what had been keeping him awake. He'd had a private funeral of sorts. Then he'd booted up his computer, done a little internet searching and completed online applications for five potential jobs in five different cities.

None of them were teaching positions.

If he couldn't be the teacher he used to be, it was time to move on. Spending time with Maggie today had shown him just how far he'd slipped. Maggie Byrne had all the vitality he'd once had— maybe more. She had the same above-and-beyond mindset, baking those ridiculously elaborate flip-flop cookies. Most important, she had the compassion—decorating her table with shoes she could then give away to the kids who needed them and even saving their pride by assuring them they were doing her a favor by taking them.

His old self would have given Maggie a standing ovation and probably shown up for the lunch distribution wearing flip-flops and scuba goggles. But what had he done instead?

He'd questioned her good sense for wasting the time.

Prof was long gone, and enough was enough. Once he found a new job, he'd give Audrey his notice and put teaching in his rearview mirror for good.

Rover, who'd been dozing on the corner of the desk, lifted his head and looked toward the cabin's front window.

"Rowr?" the cat inquired sleepily.

Headlights raked the room as a car rolled up the driveway. Neil frowned and stood. Somebody must have taken a wrong turn.

Then he heard the screaming.

He had the door open before Maggie had finished struggling up the steps, a shrieking Oliver in her arms.

"He's been like this for hours," she gasped. "I can't get him to stop. I'm sorry. I know it's late, but I just… I didn't know what else to do."

Oliver was hoarse, but he was still screaming, his eyes squinched tightly shut. Neil gently lifted the sweaty little body out of Maggie's arms.

"Come on, buddy," he murmured, settling the boy against his chest. "What's the matter?"

At the sound of Neil's voice, Oliver halted in midscream. He opened his puffy eyes a slit. Then he started to sob quietly against Neil's T-shirt.

Neil rubbed the little boy's back and shot a questioning glance at Maggie. She stood on his porch, wearing an oversize shirt and stretchy pants, her hair disheveled. She was barefoot, he noticed, and for once, she wasn't smiling. In fact, she looked as if she were about five seconds away from crying herself.

"That's the first time he's stopped screaming since we left you at the high school," she whispered.

"You'd better come in." Neil stepped inside and nodded toward the couch. Maggie sat, tucking one leg underneath her, her shoulders slumped and her eyes fixed on Oliver.

Neil sank onto the recliner. He straightened the little boy's rumpled pajama shirt, sprinkled with bright blue and red dinosaurs, and rocked the chair with one foot, patting Oliver's back in rhythm. "Everything's all right, bud," he murmured. "Let's just calm down a little, okay?"

Oliver hiccuped and stuck a thumb in his mouth, sucking noisily. Except that sound and the child's snuffly breaths, the room went still.

Maggie watched them, her eyes shadowed. "He

wouldn't stop," she repeated softly. "He cried all the way home from the high school, and even Ruby couldn't calm him down. We tried everything we could think of, but he just kept asking for you. He was hysterical, and Ruby thought... She said I should bring him here. I was desperate, so I did. I'm sorry."

"Don't apologize."

Maggie snorted a humorless laugh. "It's the least I can do after banging on your door at two in the morning. You were probably asleep—"

"I wasn't."

"And Oliver's my responsibility, not yours. Neil, I promise you, we really did try everything, but if you feel like you need to report this, I understand. I plan to talk to Mrs. Darnell myself as soon as I can get an appointment with her."

She thought he was going to report her for coming to him for help. The realization chilled him. The most horrible thing was, before his wake-up call today, he might have actually done it.

"Relax, Maggie. A woman who's willing to do whatever it takes to calm down her little boy isn't the kind of mom who needs reporting."

She nodded, looking relieved. "Is he falling asleep?"

Neil checked the toddler's flushed face. Oliver's eyelids were drooping. "I think so. Give it a minute."

"I probably made things worse, bringing him here." Maggie shook her head. "What am I going to do the next time this happens? Come banging on your door in the middle of the night again?"

"If you need to." Neil settled more comfortably in the chair. Oliver's eyes flickered at the movement, and his fingers clamped on to Neil's T-shirt. "It's okay," he murmured. Oliver seemed to be trying his best to stay awake, but the poor kid was obviously exhausted. The lids drooped again, and the child made a fretful noise, nestling closer.

Instinctively, Neil adjusted his hold, putting both arms around the little boy, snugging him in tight. That seemed to do the trick. He sighed deeply and relaxed against Neil's chest.

"I think he's almost out—" he murmured, looking up. Then he stopped short.

Maggie was crying silently, her fingers pressed over her face, her hunched shoulders shaking.

"Whoa." He had an irrational wish to put an arm around her and pat her back the way he'd been patting Oliver's. He couldn't budge, though, not without waking the child, and anyway, that probably wouldn't be…appropriate. "Hey, Maggie. It's all right."

She wiped her eyes with the back of her hand and inhaled a shuddering breath. "No," she whispered. "It isn't. Oliver's not attaching to me. Not at all. I thought it was because of his trust issues, you know? Poor Sierra… She was struggling so hard just to keep her head above water, there wasn't anything left over for her baby. I told myself it would just take time to rebuild that part of his heart. But now—" she shook her head sadly "—I don't know. He sure seems able to trust you. It doesn't make *sense*."

"No," Neil agreed quietly. "It doesn't."

She glanced at him, and her brow wrinkled. "I'm sorry, Neil. I didn't mean to sound… I'm sure you're a very nice person." She didn't seem sure at all. "It's only… Oliver just met you, but he screamed half the night for you. I've spent every minute I could with him for weeks, and he's still running away from me every chance he gets. I'm just confused and frustrated, that's all."

"You have every right to be." Neil looked down at the wispy hair tickling his chin, acutely aware of the toddler's warm weight against his chest. "This doesn't mean anything, Maggie." He spoke to himself as much as to her. More, maybe. "You're right. Oliver barely knows me. This… whatever it is…isn't based on anything real. That's why it came on so fast—because there's nothing to it. Maybe what you're building with Oliver is taking more time because it's genuine."

She was listening, her head tilted to one side, her face still wet with her tears. "I hope you're right."

"I am. I haven't done anything to deserve Oliver's trust. You have. Sooner or later that'll click in his little brain, and everything will turn around. You'll see."

"Maybe, but we don't always get what we deserve, do we?" She was watching him closely now, and she seemed to be choosing her words carefully. "Life's not like that. God's plan can be pretty mysterious. Sometimes bad things happen to us that we don't deserve. Sometimes that flips around, and we get a blessing we haven't earned. Like tonight." She smiled slightly. "I know I was kind of chilly with you when we left the school. I sure didn't deserve for you to be such a good sport when I banged on your door at two in the morning, carrying a screaming toddler—who's drooling all over your shirt, by the way. You're actually a pretty great guy, Neil Hamilton."

I used to be. He wanted to tell her that. He hadn't cared much what anybody thought of him in years, but for some reason, he wanted this woman to know that once upon a time he had been a different kind of guy. The sort of guy she would have liked.

Instead he said, "That probably just proves you don't know me any better than Oliver does."

Rover, who'd been sitting in the bedroom doorway, left his post and stalked into the living room. He jumped on the couch next to Maggie and then curled up in her lap, purring loudly. Maggie studied Neil as she stroked the cat. "Well, I'll tell you what I do know. You've been an answer to prayer for me tonight, and I'm thankful."

An answer to prayer. He flinched, and Oliver stirred in his sleep and made a fussy noise.

"Maybe we should stop talking," Neil murmured gruffly, "and let Oliver get deeply enough asleep so that you can take him back home."

"Oh," Maggie whispered with an embarrassed nod. "You're probably right. I'll shut up."

She kept looking at him, though, so Neil closed his eyes, hoping to discourage any further conversation. If he got drawn into a discussion with Maggie about God, that would prove once and for all to her that he wasn't the great guy she thought he was.

The room went silent except for Oliver's soft breathing, the tiny squeaks of the recliner as they rocked and the ridiculously loud purrs coming from the cat. Slowly, Neil's tense muscles unclenched.

This was…nice. Way back in the furthest reach of his brain, a realization dawned. He'd missed just *being* with somebody, not talking, but just sitting together, hearing her breathe and stir gently, feeling her presence. His grief had sliced at him from a thousand different directions, but until this moment, he hadn't realized how much he'd

missed simply being relaxed and quiet with another human being.

Something deep inside of him uncoiled, and a
strangely comforting current of exhaustion flowed
over him, washing away worries and troubling
memories alike. Neil leaned his cheek against the
top of Oliver's head, and for the first time in a
long, long time, he drifted effortlessly into sleep.

Well, everybody in the room was asleep but
her. Maggie stroked the dozing cat as she watched
the pair dozing in the recliner. She supposed she
should get up and try to disentangle Oliver from
Neil's arms, but she hated to.

The two of them looked so peaceful.

In spite of her relief that Oliver's scream-fest
had finally ended, seeing the little boy she loved
cradled in Neil's muscled arms made her sad.
She'd have cheerfully given anything she owned
to have Oliver cuddle against her like that.

Maggie couldn't help but remember something
Mrs. Darnell had said. Because of Oliver's past,
she felt that the ideal situation for him would be
a stable, two-parent adoptive family, not a single
mom like Maggie. The social worker had trot-
ted out statistics showing how young boys tended
to do better with fathers in the home. Maggie's
older brothers could certainly provide some posi-

tive male presence in Oliver's life, Mrs. Darnell agreed. But that still wasn't the *best* option.

To start with, Maggie hadn't been too worried. In the world of foster care, perfect situations were hard to come by—she knew that firsthand. Anyway, she and her brothers had done just fine being raised by a single foster mom. Ruby had been enough, and somehow, with God's help, Maggie would find a way to be enough for Oliver, too.

But now she wondered. There was something awfully sweet about the picture they made, Oliver and Neil. The toddler in his new dinosaur pajamas, Neil with his glasses slipped down to the end of his nose, snoring softly, his strong arms cupped protectively around the toddler.

Maybe Oliver was going to be missing out on more than she'd realized, not having a dad in the picture.

A flicker outside the cabin's side window caught her eye. A circle of light was bobbing up the path leading from the farmhouse. She sucked in a horrified breath.

Ruby. It had to be.

Maggie scooped Rover off her lap and deposited the annoyed feline on the sofa cushion. She slipped out to wait on the moonlit porch as Ruby walked slowly to the house.

"Ruby Sawyer!" Maggie scolded in a whisper as soon as her foster mother was within earshot.

"What on earth do you think you're doing, walking all this way in the middle of the night? You ought to be in your bed asleep!"

Ruby was breathing heavily, but she gave a low, comforting chuckle as she switched off her flashlight. "Oh, I've made that walk a thousand times. I could do it blindfolded. There was no way I could go to sleep not knowing how that baby was doing. Did he calm down all right once you got here?"

Ruby had always had a mind of her own, and Maggie knew from experience there was no point arguing with her. Still, she hoped Logan didn't find out about his foster mother's middle-of-the-night walk. If he did, Maggie would never hear the end of it. "Come see for yourself." She eased the door open and beckoned Ruby into the cabin.

Ruby looked down at the sleeping pair and clucked under her breath. "My, my. Ain't that something? Poor young fella. It just breaks my heart."

Maggie frowned. "But Oliver seems all right now, doesn't he?"

"I wasn't talking about our boy, honey." The elderly woman retrieved a crocheted throw from the couch and began tucking it around the sleeping figures.

"What are you doing? I need to get Oliver up and take him home," Maggie protested.

"No, baby. Leave the child here tonight. You

can come back first thing in the morning and get him."

Maggie stared. "I can't do that," she managed finally.

"Sure you can. They're both sound asleep, and it'd be a real shame to disturb 'em." Ruby stroked Oliver's hair with a gnarled finger. "Sometimes a nice, long rest is the Lord's best medicine."

"But what would Mrs. Darnell say?" Maggie whispered, worried.

Ruby flapped an indifferent hand. "Leave Ellen Darnell to me. I'll settle her if she kicks up any ruckus, not that I think she's likely to. Neil's one of Audrey Aniston's teachers, so she'll have checked him out good and proper. That woman'll know what kind of toothpaste this man uses, you can trust me on that. He's safe enough." When Maggie hesitated, Ruby added, "He *needs* this tonight, honey. This could be what starts his heart healing. I feel it in my bones."

Maggie had intended to argue, but she stopped short. When Ruby Sawyer felt something "in her bones," she was nearly always right.

"All right," Maggie agreed reluctantly. "I'll drive you home and come back to get Oliver in the morning."

"Good." Ruby allowed Maggie to steady her arm as they walked toward the door. "I ain't as young as I used to be. I'm not sure my old legs could've made a second trip down that trail tonight." The older woman paused, glancing around the sparsely furnished room and clucking her tongue. "Lives a lonely life from the look of it, don't he?" She edged away from Maggie and examined the shelves. "No pictures of family nor friends. No little mementos. Nothing but books." A cardboard box sat at the foot of the bookcase, its flaps neatly folded in. Ruby leaned over and opened it.

"Ruby!" Maggie fussed in a whisper. Casting a worried glance at the recliner, she hurried over. "Don't snoop."

"Mighty pretty, ain't she?" Ruby picked up a framed photograph and tilted it in Maggie's direction.

A dark-haired woman smiled up from the picture. "She's beautiful. Now, please, put that back, and let's go."

Ruby leaned over to rummage through the box. "No more pictures," she announced after a second. "Just a lot of degrees. Master of this, master of that. Lots of awards, too. Neil's a real smart fellow, looks like, and people think right highly of him."

"We shouldn't be nosy, Ruby. This stuff is personal. If he wanted people to see it, he'd have it out on the shelves, now, wouldn't he?" Maggie took the photo from her foster mom's hand. She put it back into the box, tucking the flaps back the way they'd been before Ruby had meddled with them.

"You're right," Ruby agreed, an odd note in her voice. "He sure don't want nobody to see these things. Seems like he don't even want to see them himself."

"They must not matter much to him, then. Come on, Ruby. If we're going, we should go."

"Oh, I don't know about that." Ruby shook her head sadly as Maggie held the door open for her. "People keep things like this out of sight for one of two reasons, child. Either they don't mean anything or they mean way too much."

"Well, whichever, it's none of our business, Ruby." She ushered the older woman through the door and closed it softly. As Ruby started down the steps, Maggie paused to peek through the porch window one last time.

The pair hadn't stirred. They slept on in the soft lamplight, snuggled under the multicolored blanket with the honeyed walls of the old cabin around them.

It was a cozy scene, but it had felt a lot cozier inside. Standing out here looking in, not so much.

"Do you really think this will help Oliver, Ruby?" Maggie asked as she started down the steps.

Her foster mom smiled. "I already told you,

honey. This ain't really about Oliver. Now let's go home and get some shut-eye. Morning'll be along before we know it, and you'll need to be fresh for your talk with Ellen Darnell."

Maggie sighed. She wasn't looking forward to that conversation. Telling the skeptical social worker Oliver had finally attached to somebody— but not Maggie—that wouldn't be pleasant.

Ruby patted Maggie's knee. "Don't you fret. God's got this, and it's going to be real interesting to see how He works it all out. Oliver will be just fine here with Neil."

"All right." As Maggie started the engine, she glanced back at the cabin one last time. In spite of the harrowing night she'd had, her lips curved up into a smile.

Spotlighted in the gleam of the headlights, Neil's keys dangled from the doorknob.

Chapter Six

Something patted Neil's nose. He drowsily lifted an eyelid to discover a pair of wide blue eyes inches from his.

"Whoa!" Neil sat up in the recliner, nearly toppling Oliver out of his lap. The little boy grabbed Neil's T-shirt to steady himself and grinned.

"Whoa!" he agreed. He tilted his head back and belly laughed. "Whoa!" Oliver repeated as soon as he could speak. This was followed by another peal of laughter.

"Well, at least you're happier this morning." Neil tried to collect his sleep-fuddled wits. Memories of the previous night trickled back. Oliver screaming. Maggie crying on his sofa. And then her comment about God that had made him close his eyes.

He must have fallen asleep. That was weird. He couldn't remember the last time he'd just drifted

off like that. He'd slept well, too. He felt ener-
gized and alert.

He couldn't remember the last time that had
happened, either.

He scanned the sun-dappled living room, doing
a status check. The clock said it was 6:00 a.m.,
and Maggie was nowhere in sight.

Since there was a toddler sitting on his lap, that
last bit was the most concerning.

The desk lamp was still burning. Everything
else was undisturbed except for an afghan pud-
dled on his knees behind Oliver.

"Where's your mom?" he wondered aloud.

Oliver's smile faded and he stuck his thumb
in his mouth. He sucked industriously, his eyes
studying Neil's face.

Neil studied him back. One of the boy's cheeks
was flushed, likely from pressing against Neil's
chest for hours, and his wispy brown hair was
standing up all over his head.

"Nice hair, kid," Neil said. "You look like you
stuck your finger in an electrical outlet."

Oliver's eyes lit back up. He didn't answer, but
around the thumb in his mouth, he offered Neil
another cheesy grin. Neil found himself grinning
back.

The kid was seriously cute, but Neil had no clue
how to take care of a toddler at 6:00 a.m. Or any
other time of day, for that matter.

"It's okay." He said the words aloud, reassuring himself as much as Oliver. "Your mom'll probably show up anytime now—bringing breakfast, unless I miss my guess. We just have to hang on until she gets here."

After thinking for a few minutes, Neil remembered a toy he'd bought for Rover on his last trip to the supermarket, a plastic ball enclosing a fuzzy mouse that squeaked when you rolled it. There was probably some rule about letting kids play with pet toys, but he hadn't taken it out of the package yet, so at least there weren't any cat germs on it. He unwrapped the ball and rolled it toward Oliver.

The child was instantly entranced and rolled it back. Neil returned it, hoping the impromptu game would hold the kid's attention until Maggie showed up. He didn't think it would be long.

It wasn't. She knocked on the door at 6:30 a.m. on the nose and walked in without waiting for an invitation, juggling a diaper bag, a plastic box and a big thermos.

"Oh, good. You're awake. I brought blueberry muffins. And diapers because I'm sure Oliver needs one by now." There was no mistaking the relief in Maggie's voice. Apparently, Neil hadn't been the only one with doubts about his toddler-wrangling capabilities.

But, hey, he'd managed all right, hadn't he?

In typical Maggie fashion, she made herself at home, walking past him into his kitchen to set down her box and the thermos. She turned and smiled brightly. "Hiya, handsome!"

Neil's eyebrows hit his hairline—about the time it dawned on him that she was talking to Oliver.

Of course.

Fortunately, Maggie was too focused on the child to notice. "How about we get you freshened up? Then we'll sit with Neil and have some breakfast together. If that's all right with you," she added, glancing apologetically at him. "I couldn't blame you if it wasn't. Sorry for leaving him here overnight. That was Ruby's idea. She walked over to check on Oliver, and she thought it best not to wake either of you up. I hope he wasn't any trouble. I worried about it all night."

Neil didn't doubt that. Maggie didn't seem quite as perky and self-assured as usual, and there were purple shadows under her eyes.

"He didn't wake up once." Neither had Neil, something he still couldn't quite believe. "Blueberry muffins sound great, don't they, buddy?"

Oliver was watching Maggie with an uncertain expression on his face, and he'd grabbed a handful of Neil's T-shirt. Her smile faltered.

Neil's professional instincts stirred. *Take charge, be nice and act like there's no question that the student will cooperate.* Over the years,

Neil had given that advice to dozens of greenhorn teachers. Most of the time, it worked.

"Okay, it's a deal. You get cleaned up while I wash my face. Then we'll eat." He loosened Oliver's fingers and stood.

Maggie fumbled in her bag for a clean diaper, her gaze fixed hopefully on Oliver. Neil stretched casually, keeping one eye on the kid. Oliver looked from Maggie to him and back. He had one hand resting against Neil's sweatpants, but he hadn't clenched on. Neil took that as a good sign.

"You guys can use my bedroom. Hurry up, 'cause I'm starving. Aren't you, Oliver?"

He didn't respond, his eyes on Maggie, who smiled at him. "We'll be real quick, won't we, sweetie? Then we'll have our muffins!"

"Sounds like a plan." As Neil moved toward the bathroom, Oliver's eyes widened with panic. The little boy took a quick step after him, looking as if he were tuning up to cry. "Go on," Neil said mildly. "Can't have dirty diapers at the breakfast table. 'Cause, seriously, buddy—whoa!"

Oliver's puckered face relaxed slightly. "Whoa!" he agreed softly.

"That's right." Neil had made it to the bathroom doorway. "Whoa! Right, Maggie?"

The woman was a quick study. "Whoa!" she agreed enthusiastically.

Oliver chuckled. "Whoa!" he repeated. Maggie laughed, and the little boy giggled again as Neil quickly shut the bathroom door.

Success.

He leaned against the thick wooden door, trying to hear, braced for screaming. He heard nothing but Maggie's musical voice murmuring something he couldn't quite make out. Then Oliver laughed again, louder.

"Whoa!"

Neil grinned. Looked like they'd pulled it off.

At the sink, he twisted the old-fashioned faucet. Removing his glasses, he splashed his face with the icy well water. When he reached for the towel, his eye caught on his reflection.

His hair was standing up on end like Oliver's, and he needed a shave—badly. His eyes weren't as shadowed as usual, though, and there were some unexpected crinkles in their corners. Friendly-looking crinkles.

Laugh crinkles.

Neil leaned in close to the mirror. For the first time in years, the man looking back at him seemed…familiar. Felt familiar, too, the way a man felt when he'd turned the corner after a long, nasty bout with the flu. As if he were finally himself again.

He blinked. He didn't have time to figure this

out now. Maggie would probably need to head to work soon.

Neil felt a twinge of disappointment at the thought, but he squashed it and yanked a pair of not-so-dirty jeans out of the hamper. He started rummaging for a different shirt, but then he paused, looking down at the dried splotch of baby drool on his chest. He snapped the hamper lid shut.

Wouldn't kill him to wear this one a little longer.

When Neil came into the kitchen, he'd changed into jeans, but he was barefoot and his hair was tousled. Maggie's heart did an impromptu somersault. The man looked disgustingly handsome for first thing in the morning. She, on the other hand, had winced when she'd caught sight of herself in the bedroom mirror. Her long night of tossing and turning hadn't been kind.

"We're all ready," she told him. "Grab some mugs, and I'll pour us some coffee."

"Thanks." He gave her a half smile, then opened a cupboard to reveal mugs upended on a bare shelf. Two. Exactly.

Maggie shook her head. She was used to Ruby's friendly kitchen, stocked with plenty of mismatched plates and cups for whatever company might happen along. Since Neil obviously had other ideas, today she'd brought along some paper plates and a sippy cup.

She set a muffin and milk in front of Oliver, who was crouched on his knees in the kitchen chair. The little boy waited until Neil sat down, then dived into his breakfast with a happy explosion of crumbs.

Maggie smiled. In spite of last night's chaos, it had been a promising morning. For the first time ever, Oliver had allowed her to change his diaper without any fuss. He'd kept saying *whoa* and giggling. Maggie had no idea what that was all about, and she didn't care. Instead of screaming, Oliver was interacting with her and making eye contact. It was a big step forward.

All that fretting she'd done last night had been a waste of time. She should've learned by now to trust God—and Ruby. Leaving Oliver here with Neil had been exactly the right thing to do.

"Thanks," Neil said as she set his steaming coffee in front of him.

"Thank *you*," Maggie said sincerely. "I really appreciate your help."

"It was no problem." Neil broke his muffin open to add a smear of butter.

Maggie studied him as she nibbled. Oliver wasn't the only one who looked better this morning. Neil looked strangely refreshed for a guy who'd spent the night dozing in a chair. Apparently, Ruby had been right on all counts. As usual.

He caught her eye and spoke around a mouthful of muffin. "Good."

Maggie smiled. She loved to see that gleam of happy appreciation in somebody's eye. "I'm glad you're enjoying it."

Neil followed the bite of muffin with coffee. "How'd you learn to cook so well?"

"Trial and error, mostly," she admitted. "Ruby let me destroy her kitchen about once a week when I was a teenager. Eventually I got the hang of it. Of course, when I went to work for Angelo, I learned a lot from him, too."

"You never went to cooking school or anything?"

"No." She tried not to feel defensive. After all, that surprise in his voice could be taken as a compliment. "There's no culinary school close to Cedar Ridge, not that I ever wanted to go to one."

He considered her over the rim of his mug. "Why not? You seem to love cooking so much. I'd think you'd want to learn all you could."

"I do. But what I want to learn, they don't teach in a classroom."

"I don't understand."

Of course he didn't. She fumbled to find the right way to express how she felt. "The thing is, I don't love cooking for the sake of cooking. I don't want to frou-frou up a plate with artistic squiggles of sauce or serve three overpriced bites of something and call it a meal. I just enjoy fixing really good, everyday food for ordinary, hungry folks. There's a difference." She made a frustrated noise. "It's hard to explain."

"I think I get what you're saying. Your focus isn't on the food itself. It's on feeding the people."

That was it. "Exactly!"

He considered her thoughtfully. Something in his expression made her feel oddly exposed, as if he were rummaging through her heart, sifting its contents. "Then I think you're right. I doubt there's anything a culinary school could teach you. One thing's for sure. There's no way they could improve on these muffins. You made the right choice."

"Well, that's a first." Maggie chuckled self-consciously. "I never thought I'd hear a teacher come out in favor of *not* going to school."

His smile mirrored hers. "I never have before," he admitted. "But then again, I've never met anybody like you before."

Their gazes held for a second, and Maggie felt her cheeks going pink. She suddenly understood why kids like Oliver resisted eye contact.

Looking into somebody else's eyes could get awfully personal.

She cleared her throat and stood. "I hate to rush off, but I have to stop by to see Oliver's social worker before I go in to work. I need to get her up to speed about everything that's been going on."

Neil rose to his feet, too. "Doesn't sound like you're looking forward to it."

"I'm not." Maggie made a wry face. She glanced at Oliver, trying to choose her words carefully. "Mrs. Darnell had reservations about this situation from the beginning, and the trouble we've been having with attachment hasn't helped. I'm concerned that when she hears about what's happened with you, it's going to make her even more doubtful that I'm the right placement." She sighed. "Who knows? Maybe she's right."

"She isn't." The quiet certainty in his voice made her cheeks warm even more. "You're the right person, Maggie. For Oliver and, I expect, for a lot of other people, too. I have a feeling you do a lot more good in this town than you realize."

"Well, thanks. I'm sure you do, too."

Her compliment didn't have quite the effect she'd hoped for. The warmth in his eyes ebbed. "Not really. I used to, maybe, before I came here. But lately, I've kind of…lost my touch."

The sad weariness on his face grabbed at Maggie's heart and gave it a painful twist. He looked so discouraged. Without thinking, she reached out and laid a hand on his arm.

"I'm sure you'll find it again," she said gently. She smiled. "I imagine you're kind of an expert on that. Most lost things usually do turn up sooner or later, don't they?"

"Most do." One corner of his mouth quirked upward, but his eyes remained sad. "But not all. I hope your meeting goes well."

She was being dismissed. Well, okay, then.

"Thank you." She turned to Oliver. "Come on, sweetie. Let's go play with the train in Mrs. Darnell's playroom!"

Maggie waited to see if her strategy would work. The electric train in the social services playroom was a huge favorite, and she'd figured it was her best chance at getting Oliver away from Neil without another meltdown.

The child looked torn, but after a second, he clambered down from the chair. "Train," he announced imperiously.

"Have fun, buddy," Neil said.

Oliver ran over and gave Neil's legs an enthusiastic hug, leaving a smear of muffin crumbs on the knee of his jeans. "Bye-bye!" The toddler headed for the door, deftly avoiding Maggie's attempts to hold his hand.

Her heart ached a little as she followed him out to the car, but she forced herself to focus on the positive. Oliver was leaving Neil without screaming. Score one for Maggie.

Or the train. Whatever. She was counting it as a win, more evidence that progress was being made.

She just hoped Mrs. Darnell agreed.

Chapter Seven

An hour later, in the Roane County Department of Social Services, Maggie described her disastrous night as honestly as she could. Mrs. Darnell tapped a pencil on her neat-as-a-pin desk as she listened while also watching Oliver through the big picture window that looked over the playroom.

When Maggie finished, the middle-aged social worker leaned back in her ancient office chair and frowned. "Well, that's concerning. Oliver *can* form bonds with people. He just doesn't seem to be forming one with you."

Maggie swallowed. "Ruby says it's a good sign—that he's attaching at all, I mean. And we have made progress, Oliver and I. It's just been really slow."

Mrs. Darnell sighed. "Yes, and the longer it takes, the worse it is for him. I don't know, Maggie. I've had doubts about this situation from the beginning. Oliver came from a traumatic situation involving a single mother, so it's understandable that he'd have a hard time bonding when he's put in a similar placement. Because of her own challenges, Sierra wasn't a dependable caregiver for Oliver, and he learned that she couldn't be trusted to meet his needs. Quite likely he's generalized that to include all women. I've wondered from the beginning if Oliver might respond better to a two-parent family, one with a father figure. His reaction to this Neil person seems to confirm that."

Maggie's heartbeat sped up. "You said there aren't any two-parent foster families open right now, though."

"True. We have a terrible shortage at the moment. But there's a group home opening up in Bartow County that might be a possibility. They have several men on staff there. I don't know if they'd take a child as young as Oliver, though."

"A group home." Maggie's heart sank. "Don't you think the individual attention Oliver's getting with me is better than that?" She struggled to keep the panic out of her voice.

It wasn't easy. Her nerves had started prickling as soon as she'd pulled into the parking lot. Her own troubled childhood was over a decade behind her now, but just the smell of this place—pine disinfectant and overboiled coffee—could make her heart start pounding. She'd experienced too many unpleasant moments here to relax.

She knew the people in the foster-care system meant well, but all too often, kids slipped through the cracks. Kids like her.

Kids like Oliver.

Mrs. Darnell's sharp blue-gray eyes softened. "Don't take my concerns as criticism, Maggie. I know you're doing everything you can, but I have to consider what's best for Oliver." She sighed. "But you're right. Group homes really aren't ideal for children Oliver's age. It's true that there aren't any two-parent families available here, but I could check with other counties—"

"But none of those other families would adopt him, would they? I mean, when all his paperwork is updated and he's eligible?"

There was a heavy beat of silence. "Probably not. Most foster families aren't pursuing adoption. But it won't be hard to find an adoptive family for a child Oliver's age, once his records are in order."

"Then he'd be uprooted all over again, wouldn't he? We both know that's not good for kids with attachment issues. Every time he's moved, it ups the risk that next time he might not attach at all."

Mrs. Darnell glanced back through the playroom window. Oliver had crouched to better watch the train. It chugged past him, and the toddler clapped his hands excitedly.

The social worker smiled, and Maggie pressed her advantage. "Ruby says if Oliver can bond with Neil that means he can form a bond with me, too. I'm already seeing some signs of it. Like this morning, he let me change his diaper without a fuss, and he made really great eye contact."

"That sounds promising," Mrs. Darnell admitted. "It's something you can build on, possibly. So this—" she checked the notes she'd scribbled on her pad "—Neil Hamilton—he's a teacher at the high school?"

"That's right."

"Audrey Aniston will have had a comprehensive background check run before she hired him." Mrs. Darnell jotted another note. "I'll just make a quick call to make sure all his clearances are current. Knowing Audrey, I'm sure they are, so we won't have to run the standard boyfriend check."

Maggie blinked. "Boyfriend check?"

"Well, that's not the official term, but yes." Mrs. Darnell set down her pen. "I'm afraid it's our policy. If you're in a relationship with this man—"

"But I'm not. We're just friends—sort of."

"Oh." The social worker frowned. "The way you talked about him, I had the impression that— Well." She shrugged. "Never mind. But in that case, how do you plan to use Oliver's attachment to this man to solve your problem?"

"I haven't…worked out all the details on that yet."

"You and Oliver will need to spend a significant amount of time with him. Do you think he'll be willing to make that kind of commitment?"

"I don't know," Maggie admitted. "I mean, he's been really nice about everything so far, but—"

"Are *you* willing to make that commitment?"

Maggie hesitated. She wasn't sure how to answer that question.

It had something to do with the way she'd felt when she'd seen Neil asleep in the recliner with an exhausted toddler sprawled across his chest and that flip-flop her heart had done when he'd walked into the cabin kitchen looking all tousled and handsome. Something about this particular man had her heart teetering on the edge of a dangerous fall. She couldn't explain it. But she could sense it.

"Maggie?" Mrs. Darnell prodded impatiently. "Are you willing to work with Mr. Hamilton or not?"

She lifted her chin. "I'm willing to do whatever it takes to help Oliver."

She meant that. When she'd decided, after lots of prayer, to start the process to foster and adopt Oliver, she'd promised herself that she wouldn't be like so many of the foster parents she'd encountered during her own childhood—the ones who'd been all warm and kind and anxious to help.

Until things got messy.

Then they'd made excuses and bailed. One right after the other.

No, she'd be like Ruby. She'd be the mom who loved without conditions, who stepped right down into a kid's mess to lift him up and who never gave up. No matter what.

So she'd had a weak-kneed moment or two over Neil. That didn't mean anything. She wouldn't let it mean anything.

"I'll ask Neil to help. I'm sure he'll say yes." Mostly sure. She'd find some way to convince him.

"Good." Mrs. Darnell nodded. "You and Oliver should spend as much time as possible with Mr. Hamilton over the next few weeks." She glanced back at her notes. "You mentioned taking Oliver along to different summer events that you're catering for your work. That's great—you can just ask Mr. Hamilton to go along. I can suggest some strategies to help with transferring Oliver's attachment to you."

"All right." Her mind ticked over the various gatherings she was scheduled to attend on behalf of Angelo's, all fun-filled, chaotic events. She couldn't picture Neil at any of them.

"I hope this works, Maggie, because if significant progress hasn't been made by the end of the summer, I'll have to find Oliver a different placement. No," she said when Maggie started to protest. "I'm sorry, but I can't let this drag on. I need to find a relationship that works for him, and fast. With at-risk children, each broken relationship is like…" The social worker trailed off, as if struggling for the right description.

"A scar." Maggie supplied the word quietly.

"Exactly. And when children are hurt in the same way over and over again, the scars build up, one on top of the other, until, finally, there's no way to get past them. We can't let that happen to Oliver."

"No, we can't." Maggie rummaged in her purse for a notepad and pen. She clicked the pen open and looked Mrs. Darnell in the eye. "And I'm not going to. Just tell me what I need to do."

Normally when Neil was at home, the phone didn't ring.

Years ago, that had been different. Back then, his phone had rung at all hours of the day and night, to the point that he'd put his cell on vibrate at bedtime so that it wouldn't wake Laura. He'd kept it close enough that it had still awakened him, though, when it had chittered in the wee hours. He'd never failed to answer it. When it came to teenagers, those middle-of-the-night calls were the ones that really counted.

Nowadays, though, his phone almost never rang, so he'd been surprised when it had buzzed twice this morning. The first time, it had been a call from the school secretary. That one had disturbed him, but it was the second call that had set him pacing the confines of the small cabin.

Maggie wanted to talk to him. She was on her way over. In fact, she should be here any minute.

And that made him antsy.

Maggie Byrne unsettled him. She stirred him up, made him feel strange and clumsy. That wasn't a good thing. Since Laura's death, he'd stayed sane by following a strict routine and keeping his feelings under tight control. But whenever Maggie came around, his carefully regimented life—and most of his common sense—took a flying leap out of the nearest window.

He pulled aside the curtains. There she was, walking up the hill through the woods, her ruddy curls sparkling in the late-afternoon sunshine. She was wearing a bright yellow T-shirt with khaki walking shorts, and she'd finished off the outfit with a pair of sturdy-looking brown hiking boots. As usual, she carried a white bakery box in her hands. She stood out against the subtle, shifting greens of the forest like a glowing beacon. When she glanced toward the cabin, he caught sight of the resolute expression on her face and winced.

He hadn't known Maggie for long, but he recognized that expression. Reminding himself of what the school secretary had told him, Neil flexed his shoulders like a boxer prepping for a match.

He met her at the door. "We should talk."

She lifted an eyebrow at his tone, but she smiled anyway. "Yes," she agreed. "We should." She lifted the box. "I brought pie."

Did this woman go anywhere without trucking along some kind of food? "Thanks, but I don't need any pie," he informed her even while he wondered exactly what kind she'd made.

"Don't be silly." Maggie snorted as she came up the steps. "Everybody needs pie." She brushed past him—she smelled like gingersnaps today— and disappeared into the cabin, leaving him standing alone on his porch.

He hesitated there for a minute, shaking his head.

She hadn't been on the premises two shakes, and he'd lost the upper hand. He was going to have to up his game.

"Neil? Do you have a pie server?" Maggie called.

He stalked to the kitchen. She was opening and closing his empty drawers, muttering under her breath. Finally she sighed and brandished a steak knife. "I guess this'll have to do. Sit down."

"I don't want pie," he repeated clearly.

"You'll want this pie." Maggie flipped up the top of the bakery box, revealing a pale green circle garnished with lime slices and mint leaves. "Although, I'll admit, it's the simplest recipe in the world. I didn't have time for anything else. Pucker pie is the first one I ever learned how to make." She paused, the steak knife poised in her hand, and glanced up at the ceiling, thinking. "I guess I was…fourteen? It's still my favorite standby in a pinch." She crunched the knife through the crust. "Go on. Sit. I'll have this ready in a second."

He smelled the sharpness of lime mingled with the scent of the gingery crust. His mouth watered. He tried to remember the last time he'd had a piece of homemade pie.

It had been a while.

"Sit," Maggie repeated. She plopped a thick wedge of the creamy pie on a plate, added a fork and slid it in his direction. She cut a smaller piece for herself before sticking the rest of it into his near-empty refrigerator.

Once seated, she picked up her fork and nipped a luscious triangle from the tip of her slice. She paused with it almost to her lips, one eyebrow raised. "You're not going to make me eat alone, are you? The calories count double that way."

Neil held out for another stubborn second, but who was he kidding? There was no way he was passing on pie. He made a frustrated noise, but he pulled out the kitchen chair and sat, trying not to notice the way Maggie's lips curved around her second bite.

"Don't expect too much," she warned. "Like I said, pucker pie's the simplest thing in the world. I do make a really mean key lime pie from scratch, though. I'll bring that another day."

He was enjoying the creamy, sweet-tart taste of the pie too much to argue with her. "Why do you call it pucker pie?" he asked, scooping up a generous second bite. "It's not sour."

Maggie laughed. There was something about the sound, something so companionable and easy that it sucker punched right in his stomach. He'd been taking a lot of blows there lately when Maggie was around.

"The first time I made it, I went a little too heavy with the lime and a little too light with the sweetened condensed milk. It was so tart it nearly turned my family's mouths inside out. My sister Torey called it pucker pie, and the name stuck. I'm glad you like it, because as usual, I'm here asking for a favor." She looked at him, her green eyes worried. "I met with my caseworker yesterday."

Oh, yeah. Neil set his fork down with a clink. "About that," he said. "I had a phone call from the school earlier, notifying me that a social worker had requested a copy of my background check. Did you have something to do with that?"

Maggie worried her lower lip for a few seconds before replying. "Yes," she admitted finally. "I hope that didn't cause you any trouble."

"The school secretary just needed my permission to share the information. I gave it." He paused, then added, "If I did anything to make you concerned about Oliver's safety with me, I wish you'd said something to me directly."

"No!" Maggie's eyes widened. "It was nothing like that. Since he's in the foster-care system, Mrs. Darnell just needed to be sure your clearances were up-to-date before she could officially approve the plan we'd come up with. I'm so sorry if we embarrassed you."

He hadn't been embarrassed. His background checks were squeaky clean. He'd been annoyed—and a little hurt that Maggie would think such a thing necessary.

Which was stupid. Of course she and this Mrs. Darnell would want to be careful. The world was a dangerous place. He understood that.

It was just that with Maggie and Oliver he'd felt more like his old self than he had in years. The phone call had been another unpleasant reminder that he wasn't anyone's beloved Prof anymore, trusted and with a reputation above suspicion.

Wait a minute. He frowned. What had she just said? "What plan?"

Maggie sighed. "It's a big ask, Neil, but please don't say no until you hear me out. First," she added, a flash of hopeful humor sparkling in her eyes, "maybe you should have another bite of pie."

Neil felt his mouth tipping up, and he steeled himself. *Don't get talked into anything foolish, Hamilton.* "What is it?"

He sensed Maggie measuring him, calculating how likely he was to say yes. She must not have liked what she saw, because she sighed again. "This may seem absurd, but the attachment Oliver's formed to you? It's important. After kids go through periods of neglect or…" She seemed to have a hard time getting the next word out. "…abuse, they often have problems trusting people. It's an emotional, knee-jerk reaction, so it's not logical. Right now, Oliver's decided to trust you instead of me. Maybe because you're a guy. Who knows?"

She sounded so genuinely bewildered that Neil felt a little insulted.

"Anyway," she went on, "the fact that he's attached at all is a hopeful sign, but we have to find some way to transfer that trust from you to me. Until then, we can't disrupt the connection he's formed with you. It could set Oliver back, Mrs. Darnell says, so that he might be afraid to connect to anybody ever again. Some kids get to that point, and it's so tragic, Neil." Suddenly, unexpectedly, Maggie reached across the table to cover his hands with hers.

Human touch, like sleep, had grown rare in Neil's life over the past few years, but Maggie offered it as generously and naturally as she'd offered her pie. The gentle warmth of her hands cupped around his made him go carefully still, and as he looked into Maggie's pleading eyes, old instincts stirred sleepily to life.

People had hurt this woman, and she still bore the scars, no matter how well she covered them up with cookies and smiles. "Did something like that happen to you?"

He sensed her reluctance to answer his question, but she nodded. "Almost. I was pretty stingy with my trust by the time I came to Sweet Springs. If it hadn't been for Ruby—" She paused and swallowed. "It almost did. And I knew kids in the foster-care system who weren't as blessed as I was. Their stories didn't end well. How could they? If you shut your heart off, if you can't love people because you're terrified of getting hurt again, what kind of life is that?"

He could have told her. He knew exactly what

kind of life that was. But she didn't seem to expect an answer, so he didn't offer one.

"I won't let that happen to Oliver," she said fiercely, "but I'm going to need your help. And who knows?" Her fingers tightened over his. "Maybe it'll help you, too. I mean, isn't it kind of providential that you're not teaching summer school this year? You said that you usually do, but if you were, you wouldn't have time for this. And you mentioned something about being out of touch. Maybe helping Oliver is part of God's plan to get you back on track with your teaching."

Neil flinched. God's plan. Right. God had given up on him a long time ago, and that feeling was definitely mutual.

This was his cue. Time to refuse politely, to back away from this personal situation and retreat into the closed-off lifestyle that kept him reasonably functional.

He'd never be Prof again. He'd accepted that. As soon as a different job came through, he'd put his teaching days behind him for good.

He knew he should make that clear. Instead, he looked into Maggie's pleading eyes, acutely aware of her fingers trembling over his. He recalled that moment in the bakery when Oliver had run to him instead of to her—and how he'd wished he could help her.

Well, now he could. She needed him. Nobody had needed him for a very long time.

"All right," he heard himself saying. "I'll try. Just tell me what I'm supposed to do."

Her eyes lit up. "I'll do better than that!" She jumped up, swiping his half-eaten pie and stashing it in the refrigerator, fork and all. "I'll show you."

Chapter Eight

Two mind-boggling hours later, Neil was sitting cross-legged on the floor of the Cedar Ridge Library beside Maggie and Oliver, participating in something called Story Time. So far, it consisted of watching the children's librarian performing a puppet show about a greedy mouse that couldn't accept a cookie without asking for endless other things. About twenty other preschoolers were seated around them, mesmerized by the gray mouse puppet bobbing around on the young woman's hand.

He loved libraries. When he'd moved to Cedar Ridge, one of his first stops had been in this quiet brick building to apply for his card. He'd visited here many times since then, but he'd never ventured into the children's area.

This was a whole different world.

The room pulsed with energy. Bright cutouts

dangled from the ceiling, murals representing scenes of children's stories decorated the walls and pint-size chairs and tables were scattered everywhere. The whole place was loud, colorful and chaotic, and Neil felt as out of place as he had when Laura had enticed him into Baby Superstore.

He snapped the lid on that memory as quick as he could, but the heartache sneaked through anyway. Just as he sucked in a quick, pained breath, the mouse requested something particularly outrageous, and the room erupted in delighted squeals. Oliver chortled and reached to pat Neil's cheek with an excited hand, pointing with the other one.

"See?" the toddler urged. "See, Neil?"

"Yeah, buddy. I see. That's silly!"

"Whoa!" Oliver supplied, nodding earnestly.

"Definitely," Neil agreed. "Whoa!"

He had to force the word past the lump in his throat. After all this kid had been through, he could still find joy in a book about a goofy mouse.

Pretty amazing, really.

The little boy scooted farther away from Maggie, settling himself in Neil's lap as the librarian turned a page, revealing even more ridiculous mouse requests. Neil felt the vibration of Oliver's chuckle against his chest, and he shot a worried glance in Maggie's direction.

She sat beside him, wearing her green Angelo's

apron. She'd explained everything on the drive over. She was booked to provide refreshments for several summer events, and she wanted him to come along to see if he could help Oliver bond with her.

He wasn't sure how to do that. Maggie was already going all out to connect with the kid. She even had a small stuffed rodent peeping from her apron's front pocket. She'd offered the toy to Oliver, but he'd ignored her.

Now she was watching him giggle in Neil's lap, her expression filled with a hungry sadness that made his heart constrict with sympathy. He knew how it felt to be the one on the outside of happiness, looking in.

She glanced up and met his eyes. Offering him a watery smile, she pressed one hand over her heart.

Thank you, she mouthed.

Neil blinked. He didn't know how to answer, so he just nodded.

He glanced from the animated story reader to the wiggling herd of children, to the moms, who all looked as if they needed a cup of strong coffee and a nap. So many patient adults, giving their time and their energy to help kids unlock the wonders of books.

Suddenly, the whole Story Time thing seemed less chaotic and more generous. Like Maggie thanking Neil for basking in an affection that rightfully should have been hers.

He rested his chin gently on the top of Oliver's head and listened as the tale came full circle, and the silly mouse asked for the exact thing he'd been given to start with.

The room broke into happy applause as the librarian announced that Angelo's bakery was sponsoring a cookie-creation event in the multipurpose room.

Maggie turned to Neil and smiled. "I'll go get everything set up. Will you take Oliver to the restroom so he can wash his hands?"

"Sure." That sounded simple enough.

It wasn't.

One advantage to being one of the few guys in the crowd was that there wasn't a line in the men's room. The disadvantage was that he was on his own when it came to figuring out how to help a toddler wash his hands at an adult-level sink. As Neil sized up the situation, the door opened behind him, and he glanced into the mirror to see Dex coming in, carrying Rory.

"'Scuse us," the boy said brusquely, elbowing past to the sink. Neil watched as Dex set his brother on the counter beside the basin. The teen squirted soap into his own palms and sudsed up Rory's hands. Then he helped Rory lean over to rinse his small fingers under the stream of water.

So that's how you do this. Relieved, Neil went to the other sink and followed suit. When he finished, he was perplexed again. The paper towels were on the other side of the sink. Was he supposed to pick Oliver up with wet hands and carry him over there?

How did parents figure all this stuff out?

"Here." Dex sullenly offered a wad of brown paper towels.

"Thanks for the help," Neil said, accepting it. "I'm a rookie."

"Huh," Dex snorted. "Sucking up to a pretty girl by being nice to her kid? That doesn't sound like such a rookie move to me, Iceman."

Neil tensed, then tossed the used towels into the trash. "Something you'd like to say to me, Dex?"

"Sure. Why not?" Dex shrugged. "You already wrecked my ticket to play ball in college. What else you gonna do? Maggie's good people, Iceman. She's helped me and little man here more than once, and we care about her. Why don't you do us all a favor and leave her alone?" When Neil started to speak, Dex held up a hand. "Uh-uh. Don't tell me you care about her, too. Everybody knows the Iceman don't care about anybody but himself."

The teenager pushed through the swinging bathroom door, leaving Neil standing by the sink.

He lifted Oliver into his arms, and the little boy grinned happily at himself in the mirror.

"Cookies now?" he asked hopefully.

"That's right." Neil forced a smile. Leaving the restroom, he followed the flow of the crowd to the library's multipurpose room.

Maggie had been busy. Cookie and mouse cutouts dangled from colorful ribbons pinned to the ceiling, and the long table was covered with green plastic tablecloths sporting Angelo's logo. A large tub of cookies sat at one end, alongside a tall stack of green paper plates. Maggie was supervising the use of piping bags stuffed with colorful icing and an amazing variety of sprinkles neatly separated into containers.

The noise was deafening, and the generous plastic tarps underneath the tables were already splattered with cookie crumbs and sprinkles.

Maggie lifted her head to scan the crowd, and Neil smiled. She'd donned a headband with brown mouse ears, and she'd drawn black whiskers on her cheeks and darkened the tip of her nose. She should've looked silly.

She didn't. She looked…sweet.

When she caught sight of them, she waved excitedly, apparently forgetting she was holding an icing bag. Blue frosting squirted down the front of her apron, making the children around her squeal delightedly. Maggie tipped her head back and laughed along with them.

She dabbed at her apron with a paper towel and beckoned.

"Hi, guys!" Maggie said cheerfully when they were close enough to hear her over the din. "Isn't this fun? Are you ready to decorate a cookie, Oliver?"

Neil felt the child's fingers tighten on the fabric of his shirt as he surveyed the chaos with an uncertain expression.

"Tell you what." Maggie indicated the spot next to her. "Why don't you stand right here so I can help you?"

Neil thought Oliver would refuse, but then the child wiggled, indicating he wanted to get down. Neil set him on the floor, and Oliver edged closer to Maggie, tugging Neil along by one finger.

Maggie helped the toddler choose a mouse-shaped cookie. She spooned bright yellow frosting into a piping bag and offered it to Oliver. Reluctantly, the little boy released his grip on Neil's thumb and squeezed the bag. Nothing happened. Maggie reached down and gently adjusted his fingers.

"Try again, sweetie."

Oliver clenched his little fist, and a huge amount of goo squirted out, half on the cookie and half on the tablecloth. He froze. He looked at

Maggie fearfully, his face puckering. She quickly dipped up a bit of the wasted frosting with her finger and dabbed it on his mouth. He licked at it, his eyes wide with surprise. His face relaxed into a grin.

"Good!" he said, happily. "Good, Maggie!"

Maggie glanced at Neil, her face alight with joy, before reaching down to tousle Oliver's hair.

"Yes, sweetie," she murmured. "Very good!"

She looked at Neil as if waiting for him to chime in. He smiled mechanically, but he didn't answer. The truth was, he was finding it a little difficult to breathe.

When Maggie Byrne smiled like that, with her heart shining in her eyes, she was…really something.

A rough nudge startled him out of his trance. Dex had shouldered his way up to the table, Rory perched in his arms.

"Move over, Iceman," the boy ordered. "You're in my way."

"Dex." Maggie's voice was softly reproachful, and the boy shot her a sheepish look. "Come here, Rory, and let's pick you out a cookie to decorate."

Dex handed his brother over and watched as Maggie led the little boy through the process of choosing a cookie and an icing color.

"There's no milk in that icing, is there?" he asked worriedly.

"Nope. I made sure," Maggie said.

Neil cleared his throat. This was as good a time as any to bring up something he'd been thinking about since Maggie had clued him in about Dex's situation.

"Dex," he said, "are you coming to the school-lunch pickup on Wednesday?"

"You'd better," Maggie interjected. "Angelo's doing a tropical-island lunch next week. Pigs in a blanket and a fancy fruit salad. It's going to be great!"

The boy smiled at Maggie. "I'll be there," he promised.

"Good," Neil said. "I'll give Principal Aniston a call and see if we can figure something out about that class you failed. Maybe you could make up the missed assignments through independent study over the summer. I'll let you know what she says on Wednesday."

Dex considered him warily. "All right." After intercepting a look from Maggie, he added, "Thanks."

"Sure."

After Dex and Rory had moved down the cookie assembly line, Maggie leaned in close. She smelled like vanilla and sweet frosting today, simple and honest and wonderfully good.

"That's really nice of you, Neil, helping Dex out like that."

"I'm not being nice," he answered quietly. "I'm trying to undo a mistake. I didn't know about Dex's situation, but I should have. I would have, if I'd been paying attention. The truth is, I haven't been pulling my weight at school for a long time, not in the ways that really matter."

He half expected Maggie to argue with him, to offer polite platitudes. She didn't. She just nodded. "Well, Ruby says once you admit there's a problem, you're halfway to solving it. I'm so thankful you're willing to help out with Oliver this summer, but I promise, we won't take up all your time. You'll need to work with Dex, too, and I don't want to be selfish."

He doubted there was a selfish bone in this woman's body. "Don't worry about that. I'll make time for Dex, but other than him, this summer I'm all yours."

He spoke lightly, casually, but at his words, something not-so-casual glimmered in Maggie's eyes—something that made his insides play musical chairs.

All she said was "Brave words from a man with yellow frosting on the tip of his nose."

"I don't think you're in any position to talk." He tweaked one of her crooked mouse ears. She flushed and smiled, and he couldn't help it. He smiled back. "Did you say Wednesday's lunch is island themed? I don't have to wear a grass skirt, do I?"

Her eyes twinkled. "Would you?"

He started to answer, then changed his mind. Better to leave those words unspoken.

If you asked me to, I don't know. I just might.

Her pink flamingos kept falling over. At lunchtime the following Wednesday, Maggie dabbed her sweaty forehead—it was blazing hot in the school parking lot—and leaned over to adjust the flock of bright plastic birds she'd scattered in the shrubbery.

"Stay *put*," she muttered.

"Bad birdie," Oliver said irritably. Then, for the dozenth time that morning, he said, "Neil?"

"He'll be along in a little bit, honey."

"Told you those things wasn't going to stay up." Angelo was setting up the lunch table with mathematical precision. "We ain't had rain lately, so the ground's too hard to jab the sticks in deep." He tugged at the necklace of plastic flowers Maggie had placed around his neck, his expression pained. "This is getting in my way." He twisted the garland around so that it dangled down his back.

Maggie ignored him and stepped around Oliver to straighten another sagging flamingo. As soon as she did, the first one flopped back over.

"Bad," Oliver repeated. Yanking off his own flower necklace, he dropped it on the ground beside the fallen bird and stomped it. "Neil!" he demanded petulantly.

"Soon, sweetie." Maggie retrieved the smooshed garland and draped it over a nearby bush. "Well, that was a waste of a dollar ninety-nine."

"What did you expect?" Angelo asked grouchily. "You always go a little overboard, but this—" He gestured at the huge paper flowers, the leaning flamingos and the multicolored ribbons fluttering around them. "It's way too much."

Maggie didn't argue. Angelo was right. She'd gone way overboard today, and not only with the decorations.

After Neil's grass-skirt joke at the library, she'd thought it would be…funny…to surprise him by wearing an island-themed outfit today. She didn't own a grass skirt, but there was something else in her closet that fit the bill perfectly.

Or so she'd thought.

Maggie tugged irritably at the dress she was wearing. Last summer, it had been her favorite thrift-store find. A rosy cranberry color, it was splotched all over with big white flowers and tied at the side of the waist, falling to an uneven hem that fluttered around her calves. Today, she'd paired it with some strappy little sandals, and she'd even picked a white hydrangea from the yard to tuck behind one ear.

It had seemed like a cute idea—until she'd sat down at the breakfast table. Ruby had raised her eyes over her coffee cup, remarking that Maggie sure was dressed fancy for passing out sack lunches.

Then she'd winked and asked if Neil was helping out again today.

Maggie had flushed. She'd received a lot of compliments on this dress last year, and yes, maybe in the back of her mind, she'd kind of liked the idea of Neil seeing her in something other than an apron and mouse ears.

Unfortunately, the dress was a little snugger than it had been last summer—all that taste-testing at the bakery added up—and the sandals had pinched angry blisters on her toes. She was donating the whole outfit back to the thrift store first chance she got. Plus, she'd put so much product in her hair that it felt stiff and weird, and like these frustrating flamingos, her hydrangea seemed determined to turn itself upside down.

Anyway, all her trouble had been for nothing, because—

"Iceman didn't show?" Dex separated from the pack of milling teenagers and strolled up to the lunch table. "Figures."

"Something came up, but he'll be here as soon

as he can." Maggie repeated what she'd been telling Oliver all morning. Neil had left a voice mail while she was in the shower. He wouldn't be able to help make the lunches, but he'd meet her at the school and help pass them out. He hadn't offered any further explanation. "Where's Rory today?"

"With our grandma." Dex looked disgusted. "She gets tired easy, and I don't leave him with her too much. But today I thought me and Iceman might need to talk about that independent-study thing, so I told Rory I'd bring his lunch back to him. He likes coming, and he was real disappointed." He snorted. "Then Iceman ain't even here. I shoulda known."

"I'm sure he'll be along any minute."

"Yeah, right."

Maggie started to argue, then glanced at her watch. It was already ten minutes past the time they usually started handing out the food.

So much for that *I'm all yours* remark the other day. She was embarrassed now to remember how her stomach had fluttered when Neil had said those words.

"We'd better get started," Angelo called. "My fruit cups ain't going to last good in this heat. Besides, I got to get back to the bakery. Inez can only handle things by herself for so long."

"Okay." When she'd explained that Neil would be late, Angelo had insisted on coming along to help. Lately, her boss had been watching her like a grouchy guard dog, ready to woof at anybody he saw as a threat. "Come on, Oliver, and help Mr. Angelo and me hand out the lunches. Won't that be fun?"

Oliver scuffed his red tennis shoes in the pine straw around the shrubbery and ignored her. Maggie couldn't help but notice the difference in the toddler's attitude. When Neil was around, he seemed so much more open, more willing to interact with Maggie.

She'd probably made things worse by assuring him that Neil would be arriving any minute. Now, if he didn't show up, it would destroy what little progress she and Oliver had made.

Fortunately, just when she was about to call the kids up, she noticed Neil's Jeep pulling into the parking lot. She breathed a grateful sigh of relief.

"Oliver," she said, pointing. "Look who's here!"

Oliver's sulky face lit up. "Neil!" He scooted down the sidewalk, making a beeline for his hero. The man knelt, and the child took a flying leap into his arms. "Neil! Neil!"

"Hiya, buddy. Sorry I'm late."

Oliver didn't answer, but he didn't have to. His beaming face made it clear that all was forgiven. Must be nice, Maggie thought, to have a little kid run like that to meet you, grinning as if you were

Christmas and summer vacation all rolled up into one human being.

As Neil walked closer, Maggie's eyes widened.

"Oh." Even getting that syllable out was tough. "Wow."

The shirt he was wearing sported huge, intensely yellow birds on a background of bright pink and purple flowers. It was a knock-your-eyes-out, look-at-me kind of shirt. On Neil Hamilton, it packed an additional punch because it was so…unexpected.

She wasn't the only one having some trouble. Neil's gaze skimmed her, and she had the satisfaction of seeing him blink hard as if to double-check his vision.

"Wow yourself," he said quietly. "You look… amazing."

"Thanks." And just like that, the dress ricocheted right back up to the top of her favorites list. Her lips curved. "*Amazing* seems to be the word of the day. I guess this solves the mystery of why you were late. Went shopping, did you?"

He gave her a slow grin. "What makes you think that?"

"That shirt isn't exactly something I'd picture hanging in your closet."

"Maybe you don't know me as well as you think you do."

"Nice try." Maggie reached out and snapped

off the price tag dangling under Neil's sleeve. She squinted at it and winced. "Ouch. Please tell me you got this awful thing on sale."

"You know, I'm starting to think you don't like my new look." He glanced down at Oliver, who was tracing a bright beak with one stubby fingertip. "You like my shirt, don't you, buddy?"

The little boy looked up at Neil, his eyes wide. "Whoa."

Neil guffawed, and Maggie laughed with him. As she did, Oliver met her eyes, his face crinkled with joy. "Whoa!" He clapped his hands and giggled. "Whoa, Maggie!"

"That's right, sweetheart." She struggled to get the words around the happy lump that had formed in her throat. "That shirt is a *whoa* if I've ever seen one."

Neil smiled at her. "It's not a grass skirt, but it's the best I could do on such short notice."

"It's perfect," Maggie assured him. "Absolutely perfect."

Chapter Nine

Neil chuckled at Maggie's choice of words. No, it wasn't perfect. It was— What was that word his prim grandmother had been so fond of?

Tacky.

He'd thought his new shirt was bright in the shady cabin, but out here in the intense June sunshine, it went way beyond that. He'd chosen it with Maggie in mind, figuring they'd have a good-natured argument about which of their shirts was the most obnoxious. Even though this was easily the most over-the-top thing he'd ever laid eyes on, he'd had no confidence that he'd win the contest. Maggie, he knew, tended to go all out.

She had again today, but she'd taken it in a whole different direction. Instead of a silly getup, she'd gone with a rosy floral dress that clung gently to her curves, and she wore her hair down in a cascade of ruddy curls. A large white flower drooped sweetly beside one ear, and she wore a matching garland around her neck.

No, today Maggie didn't look silly at all. She looked incredible.

The woman standing in front of him sure didn't belong in a high school parking lot. She belonged on some tropical beach at sunset. He could picture her walking along the surf while seagulls dipped over the ocean, catching the last of the light on their wings. He saw the scene clearly in his mind's eye… Maggie, sandals dangling from one hand, laughing up at the man she loved, bumping into him playfully as she dodged a wave.

Knowing Maggie, she'd smell like coconut macaroons, and she'd have packed a picnic lunch.

"Neil? Is everything okay?" He blinked. Maggie was looking at him funny.

"What? Oh, yeah. Absolutely." *If you don't count the fact that every time I look at you in that outfit, I feel like a boxer just sucker punched me in the stomach.*

He couldn't remember the last time he'd felt so bowled over by a woman.

No, that wasn't true. He remembered, all right.

It had been an ordinary day, and he'd been running late, as usual. He'd strode out to his car, coffee in hand, leather case full of graded papers slung over one shoulder. He'd glanced back and seen Laura standing in the doorway, her hands cupped over her rounded belly.

Slow down, Prof, she'd called. *You're forgetting something.*

He'd grinned and jogged back up the steps to kiss his wife goodbye. And for a second, looking down into her face, he'd felt…awed. Standing there on the doorstep, Neil had thanked God with his whole heart for the blessings he'd been given.

Now get to work. Laura had given him a playful push. *Those kids aren't going to teach themselves.*

So he'd left for school—his wallet forgotten on the bedside table. And the next time he'd seen Laura—

He flinched from the memory. "I guess we'd better get to work," he said abruptly. "Am I on drink duty again?"

Maggie shot a look at the table. Angelo was presiding behind it, swathed in a large apron, his bald head perspiring.

"The kids can get their own drinks today. Angelo's got some sort of glitch with the fruit salad, and he needs you to help him. Oliver?" She looked hopefully at the boy, perched on Neil's forearm. "Want to come stand with me at the front of the line?"

She held out her hands, but Oliver frowned and laid his head against Neil's chest. "Neil," he said firmly.

"All right." Maggie's hopeful expression faded into resignation. "You can help Neil. Angelo—" She lifted her voice. "No yelling, okay? Not at the kids, not at Neil. I mean it." Angelo's only response was an irritated wave. Maggie lowered her voice and leaned close to him. She did smell like coconut—mixed with something spicy and sweet. "Have fun," she murmured wryly. She beckoned to the students. "Come and get it, guys!"

Neil moved behind the table to stand beside Angelo. He set Oliver next to him on the ground, and the toddler became absorbed with playing with one of the big plastic flamingos in the shrubbery.

"So?" Neil asked pleasantly. "What's the problem with the fruit salad?"

The older man shot him a narrow look. "I yell at you, you gonna get your feelings hurt?"

Neil shrugged. "You can yell if you want to. It won't bother me, but it won't get these lunches fixed any faster, either." He surveyed the setup—large plastic platters full of bite-size treats. "This is different from last time."

"It's like a sack-lunch buffet," Angelo explained gruffly. "I thought it'd be a nice change and cut down on waste. The kids get to pick what they want to put in their bag. I got ham rolls and pigs in a blanket and grilled pineapple bites with bacon, and I got four different flavors of chips. Now, that right there in those little cups is the ambrosia fruit salad, and that's our problem. Inez, my part-time help at the bakery, forgot to put the cherries in. She can't help forgetting stuff. She's old." He nudged a big jar of maraschino cherries toward Neil, along with a spoon. "You're gonna fix 'em. Open them up and put a cherry in, then snap 'em closed again. Think you can manage that?"

Neil frowned. The little cups were already capped and stacked. Seemed a waste of time to open them all up just to add one additional bit of fruit. "Why—?"

"My ambrosia always has cherries!" Angelo interrupted loudly. He shot an apprehensive look at Maggie, who was marshaling the students into a line. "If I was serving these fruit cups at the bakery, I'd fix 'em right, so we're going to fix 'em here. These kids ain't got much, and Angelo's ain't giving them a sloppy lunch." The older man jutted his chin out as if daring him to argue.

Neil grinned. What had Maggie called her surly employer? *Big old ball of mush.* Looked like she was right.

"You're the boss. You say everybody gets a cherry, then everybody gets a cherry."

"You might have a little sense after all," Angelo grunted grudgingly. "Now stop talking and get working, smart guy. Thanks to you, we're running late." The bakery owner wrinkled his nose. "And just so's you know, that shirt wasn't worth it."

Neil unscrewed the lid of the cherry jar without answering. He hadn't corrected Maggie when she'd assumed that he was late because he'd been buying this obnoxious shirt. The truth was, he'd bought the shirt on the way home from Story Time at the library.

He'd been late this morning because he'd had a virtual interview for one of the jobs he'd applied for online.

It had been a weird experience, interviewing over the internet, but as near as he could tell, it seemed to have gone well. The guy on his computer screen had ended the meeting by praising the curriculum company he worked for, and Neil figured that wouldn't have happened if there wasn't going to be a job offer upcoming.

That was good news because it was a primo job. Nice pay, excellent benefits, located in Charleston. He'd be developing history curriculum for high schools, and if teaching was off the table, that was a pretty sweet second choice.

The guy doing the interview had frowned when Neil hadn't had any questions—and he'd devoted a few additional minutes to upselling his company. Neil could've saved him the time. His hurry to finish the interview hadn't had anything to do

with doubts about retirement benefits or vacation days.

He hadn't liked the idea of keeping Maggie
waiting—of disappointing her.

"This ain't rocket science." Angelo interrupted
Neil's thoughts. "Speed it up. You're making folks
wait."

The older man had a point. The line was moving along quickly, and he was getting behind on
cherry duty.

"You showed up after all." Neil glanced up to see
Dex across the table, two lunch sacks in his hands.

"Yep. Here." Neil wiped his sticky fingers, then
dug in his pocket and produced a folded piece of
paper. "I roughed out what you need to do to make
up the work you missed. It's all on this paper,
along with my email address and my cell number. I've cleared it with Principal Aniston, and
we're good to go."

Dex unfolded the paper and looked at it in-
credulously. "Seriously? I do the stuff on this list,
I'll pass?"

"That's the deal. You can pace the work to suit
yourself—as fast or as slow as you want. If you
have any problems with the assignments, just give
me a call and we'll hash it out." Neil held two
containers toward Dex, then snatched them back.
"Hang on a minute. Angelo—any milk products
in this?"

"Nope."

Neil offered the cups to Dex. "All good."

The boy accepted them and placed them in his sacks. Neil's eyes moved to the next kids in line. Almost everybody had collected their lunches now.

Which was a good thing. He was almost out of cherries, and he didn't want to face Angelo if he gave out a serving of fruit salad without one. He glanced back to find that Dex hadn't budged. The boy met his eyes with an impressive intensity.

"Look, Iceman. I don't know if you're just helping me to impress Maggie or what. But I ain't playing around, and I need to know you aren't. I *need* to pass this class."

Neil met his gaze squarely. "I'm not playing, Dex. I'll help you. I should have helped you before. I didn't know about— I didn't know."

Dex nodded shortly. "I guess we'll see, then. I'm going to do my part. You got my word on that. I know I've messed stuff up in the past, but now that I have Rory to look after, I need to get things right. When you got a little kid like him, who looks up to you, it makes a difference. You'll do anything it takes."

Neil's eyes dropped to Oliver, who was having a staring contest with a flamingo, and then flickered over to Maggie. She was fiddling with the flower in her hair while she talked to the last couple of girls in line. "Yeah. I can understand that."

"Dex, hurry up. You're blocking the drinks," a kid complained.

Dex moved on, but Neil noticed that he halted at the end of the table and carefully refolded the paper. He stowed it in his pocket before heading down the sidewalk with his lunches.

When the last kids had been served, Maggie walked over.

"Great job! Angelo, the kids loved the buffet idea. All that's left is cleanup, and we're done. Oliver, want to help me gather up all the birdies?"

He considered her for a minute, and his eyes slid over to Neil.

"I'm going to be cleaning the tables with Mr. Angelo," Neil pointed out. "Boring."

"Birdies," Oliver decided. Maggie beamed, and he felt that sucker punch hit his gut again.

The woman sure was beautiful when she smiled like that.

He watched the two of them wander along the shrubbery, picking up the leaning flamingos. Maggie carried on an animated conversation. Oliver wasn't answering, but he seemed to be listening.

"You gonna help or you just gonna stand there?" Angelo asked.

"Sorry." Neil reached under the table for the

coolers they'd stashed. He popped one open and started stowing away the few leftovers.

"I wasn't too sure about you," Angelo said after a minute, "but maybe you're all right. That little one there—" he jerked his chin in Oliver's direction "—he's a lot like me. He don't take to many people." The baker paused. "He likes you."

"I like him, too."

"It's a good thing you're doing, helping Maggie with him."

"I'm enjoying it." That was true, Neil realized with surprise. He'd had fun picking out this absurd shirt. Setting up that independent study for Dex had felt pretty good, too.

"She's worked for me since she was fifteen, Maggie has." Angelo thumped the lid down on a cooler. "She drives me up a wall half the time, but she's the closest thing to family I got. The way I see it, you help Maggie out, you help me out. So, you come by Angelo's anytime, and you'll get your coffee for free."

Neil lifted an eyebrow. "You don't have to do that."

"You don't have to do what you're doing, neither. I just got two conditions."

"What's that?"

"First, you don't tell Maggie. She already has me giving away food to half this town, telling people how sweet I am." Angelo made a disgusted noise. "If she finds out about this, I'll never hear the end of it."

Neil grinned. Angelo was probably right. "Fair enough. What's the second condition?"

"Don't wear that shirt in my bakery. You do, and forget about free—I'm charging you double. It gives me a headache. Why'd you buy that ugly thing, anyhow?"

Neil glanced at Maggie. She was laughing at something Oliver had done, and she touched the tip of his nose with a playful finger.

"Maggie put the idea in my head," he admitted. "She has a knack for talking people into things."

Angelo barked a laugh and slapped Neil on the back so hard that the spoon he was holding clattered down onto the table.

"Tell me about it," the old man murmured as he bent to pick up another cooler.

Three days later, Maggie lugged the canvas case holding Angelo's new event tent out across the lush grass of Cedar Ridge's Puppy Park. Oliver walked beside her, clutching a sippy cup of milk.

"Neil?" the toddler asked hopefully for the tenth time since she'd buckled him in the van that morning.

"He'll be here, sweetie. Any minute."

"Okay." Oliver nodded earnestly. "In a minute." He reached out and took Maggie's free hand. Startled, she glanced down. The toddler trudged ahead, swigging his cup, as if holding her hand wasn't any big deal.

Except, of course, it was.

Maggie blinked back tears. Oliver had come such a long way. They weren't there yet, but these little improvements happened more and more frequently—especially, she noticed, when there was a prospect of seeing Neil.

Oliver hadn't shown much interest in coming today, not even when she'd mentioned the dogs— until she'd told him that Neil would be there. Then the little boy had hopped up from the kitchen table, hooting happily.

He sure brightens up when he hears Neil's name, doesn't he? Maggie had asked Ruby wistfully.

Ruby's faded eyes had twinkled. *He ain't the only one, I notice.*

Maggie had shot her foster mother an exasperated look. *Don't start being silly.*

Silly? Ruby had sipped innocently from her coffee mug. *Oh, no. I wouldn't want to be silly. So, you gonna wear a pretty dress to this shindig, too? Or do you only dress up fancy to pass out sack lunches?*

Maggie had stuck out her tongue and quietly changed her plans to wear her new blouse. Instead, she went for a simple T-shirt and shorts. She even painted a goofy paw print on one cheek just so Ruby would know there was absolutely nothing *silly* going on.

And there wasn't. Sure, she liked Neil Hamilton. How could she not? He was a very kind man who was going out of his way to help her. And yes, maybe she'd had a few romantic thoughts about him, but they didn't mean anything. How could they? She wasn't looking for a relationship, and even if she was, she couldn't afford to complicate her life right now. Besides, she and Neil were so different—he was all scholarly and bookish, and she hadn't taken a class since high school. He'd never be interested in somebody like her, so Ruby might as well get that hopeful gleam out of her eye.

Maggie dumped the case next to the folding chairs and the plastic tub of cookies she'd already unloaded. Treasuring the feel of Oliver's little hand clutching hers, she surveyed the pretty fenced park.

The official opening of the Cedar Ridge Puppy Park was scheduled for 10:00 a.m., and some pet owners and their dogs had already arrived to wait for the advertised celebration. A small grandstand, festooned with red, white and blue bunting, had been set up for the mayor's speech. The local vet was offering free rabies vaccinations, a photographer was setting up a backdrop to photograph people's pets, and another vendor was busy unboxing colorful dog toys. At Maggie's suggestion, Angelo's had signed on to offer free bottled water and cookies to all comers.

For once, Angelo had given in without the usual fuss, agreeing that it would be good publicity and Oliver would enjoy watching the dogs. Then, in an all-too-casual tone, he'd asked if "that teacher fellow" would be going along, too. When Maggie had shot him a suspicious look, he'd hastily pointed out that the coolers would be heavy. She'd need help carrying them.

Well, that was true enough—the filled coolers weighed a ton. They were waiting in the van. Angelo had made her promise not to try to unload them herself.

In the meantime, she'd get the tent set up. The temperature was predicted to climb into the nineties, and they'd need the shade. Maggie loosened the ties of the vinyl pouch and pulled out the instructions.

Fifteen minutes later, when the green monster fell on her head for the fourth time, she dropped to the ground beneath it with a frustrated yell.

"Simple three-step process, my *foot*!"

"Maggie?" Neil lifted a corner of the collapsed tent and peered under it. "You all right?"

She stared grimly back at him. Oliver stood beside his hero, grinning from ear to ear.

"Tent go boom!" he announced. "Whoa!"

Neil grinned. "You said it, Oliver. Come on, Maggie.Let's get you out of there." Shoving the tangled metal supports and fabric aside, he reached to help her up from the damp grass.

Her heart gave a skip at his touch, which compounded her irritation.

Down, girl, she told herself firmly. *None of that allowed. Remember?*

"This tent is defective," she announced with a frustrated grimace. "I followed the instructions to the letter, but it won't stay up."

"Then let's forget the instructions and see if we can figure this out on our own." Neil examined the collapsed tent. "Looks like we just need to get the legs positioned and push the top up."

"I tried that."

"Really? Well, let me take a shot at it." Quickly, he pulled the four legs into position and ducked under to fiddle with the center of the tent.

Oliver started to follow, but Maggie snagged the straps of his little overalls and held him still. "Stay out here, sweetie," she murmured when he protested. "The tent's about to go boom again."

"I heard that." Neil's answer was muffled under the droopy canopy. "Actually, I think I've got it. I just have to push this center piece straight…"

"Be careful with that one," Maggie warned. "It—"

"Ouch!"

"—pinches," she finished.

"This is a two-person job," Neil said. "If we push all of these joints straight at the same time, it should pop right up. I need an extra pair of hands."

"The ad promised this was a *one*-person job. Wait till they see the review I leave on this useless thing. Hang on a minute, Neil." Maggie tugged over the plastic tub of cookies and patted its flat top. "Sit on this, Oliver, and you can see Neil and me make the tent go up. Or boom. Either way, it'll be fun to watch. Okay?"

"Okay!" Oliver plopped his bottom obediently on the lid of the tub, his eyes wide with anticipation.

"Stay right there, sweetie. Neil, I'm coming in." Maggie ducked beneath the fabric.

The space inside the half-collapsed tent was dim and smelled overpoweringly of new vinyl. Neil stood in the middle, his head poking against the top of the fabric as his hands explored one of the folding hinges. The sunlight filtering through the fabric gave his skin a greenish tint, and his glasses had slid to the end of his nose. He squinted through the lenses, his perspiring brow wrinkled with concentration.

Not anybody's best look, so there was no logical reason at all for Maggie's heart to be doing all kinds of gymnastics as she edged closer.

It did them anyway.

"I owe you an apology." He cut her a sideways glance, a corner of his mouth tipping up ruefully. "I don't know why I thought I had a better shot at getting this up than you did. When they passed out know-how on putting stuff together, I must've been camped out in the remembering-useless-historical-trivia department. I stink at this stuff."

A man who'd admit when he wasn't good at something. Maggie's heart did another round of acrobatics, and her stomach added a slow flip and roll, sending an explosion of girlie flutters all the way up to her throat.

Neil Hamilton might be her kryptonite.

She'd spent the first half of her childhood dodging her mother's boyfriends—angry, insecure men who had plenty of weaknesses but never admitted to them. She'd spent the second half with three tight-lipped foster brothers, boys who'd come to Ruby's house from unimaginably hard places. She loved each of them beyond reason, but more than once, their testosterone-fueled chest beating had driven her to spray them down with the garden hose.

And then run for dear life.

But this guy, who tossed off jokes about his lack of mechanical abilities and his absentmindedness? Neil, with his smudged glasses and his rumpled hair, who had a soft spot for stray cats? This quiet man with the pain etched deeply into his face, who'd open his door to women and screaming toddlers in the wee hours of the night?

He was a different matter altogether.

Since the minute Oliver had entered her life, she'd been determined to keep her focus on him. She had no time for romance, but right now she was finding Neil… What was the word her fuddled brain was looking for?

Irresistible.

God, please. I can't fall for Neil Hamilton. I know Ruby's been pestering You about my love life, but let's be reasonable. He's all bookish and serious and brilliant, and I cry over sappy commercials and bake cookies for a living. Besides, he's obviously carrying a lot of baggage, and my chances to adopt Oliver are shaky enough as it is. The last thing I need right now is a fixer-upper boyfriend. Help a girl out here.

"Let's give this a shot," Neil said, interrupting her frantic prayer. "You push those two hinges straight. I'll get these two, and we'll see what happens. On three. One…two…*three*!"

Maggie pushed up with all her might. She heard a snap, and then the entire tent collapsed completely around them. The folding supports whopped her firmly on the back, propelling her forward. She stumbled against Neil's chest, and his arms went around her, steadying her.

"Well," he murmured, "that did not go according to plan."

Maggie blinked at him. She was standing way too close, so close she could smell the spicy scent of his shampoo. For the life of her, she couldn't think of even one reasonably coherent thing to say.

"Sorry." His mouth quirked up at the edges. "You can't say I didn't warn you."

She didn't answer. Her brain had spiraled into full-blown overload. She and Neil were enclosed in a misty green envelope, and the rest of the world had just…vanished. She looked up at him mutely.

His eyes crinkled behind his crooked glasses, but then, as their gazes held, the humor ebbed from his face. As the seconds edged into a long moment, the friendliness in his expression was replaced by something that made her hammering heart shift into an entirely different gear.

"Maggie." The last functioning bit of her brain registered that his voice sounded a little ragged around the edges. "Maggie, I—"

A wash of blinding light made both of them blink. Maggie's brother Logan peered under the edge of the sagging tent.

"You all right, Mags?" Logan's sharp gaze

shifted between Maggie and Neil. "I saw the tent go down, and I came over to check on you. Don't just stand there. It's like an oven under this thing. Come out before you have a heatstroke." He grabbed Maggie's arm and tugged her into the open.

Neil followed, batting the heavy material out of the way. Once both of them were clear, Logan released the tent, which toppled onto the grass.

"Whoa!" Oliver observed from his seat on the cooler. The little boy's eyes were as big as saucers.

"I've got to agree with you, buddy. That was definitely a whoa-worthy moment." Neil's eyes met Maggie's, and for a split second, she wondered if he was talking about the tent collapse or something else. He turned to survey the crumpled canopy. "I think I broke it."

"Looks that way." Logan scanned Neil from head to toe with what the family called his law-and-order look on his face. In another minute, he'd be asking to see some ID. Maggie cleared her throat. Logan's gaze cut to her, and his right eyebrow lifted.

What's going on here? She heard the question as plainly as if Logan had spoken aloud.

Caught between Neil and her brother, Maggie felt annoyingly flustered. She forced a smile. "I think it was broken when I got it."

"If it wasn't, it is now," Logan drawled. She

sent him a dirty look, but her brother paid no attention. He crossed his muscled arms over the tan sheriff's uniform. "You must be Hamilton."

"Neil." He extended his hand. Maggie's eyes narrowed when Logan waited a few seconds before accepting the courtesy.

"Logan Carter. I'm Maggie's overprotective big brother. One of 'em, anyway."

"And the county sheriff," Neil observed. Maggie gave him credit. Unlike most people, he didn't seem intimidated by Logan.

"That's right." Logan's expression didn't soften. "What are you doing here today, Hamilton, besides knocking down tents on top of my sister's head?"

"Helping," Maggie said clearly. Judging from the look on Logan's face, she'd better get back in this conversation before he challenged Neil to an arm-wrestling contest or something equally foolish. "Speaking of that." She rummaged in her purse and pulled out her key ring. "Would you mind bringing the coolers of water over from the van, Neil?"

"Sure." He took the key and started toward the parking lot. Oliver jumped up and followed. Maggie watched as Neil took the toddler's hand, slowing his pace so Oliver could keep up.

"Tent went boom," Oliver said cheerfully.

"Yep," Neil agreed. "Turns out I'm not so good at tents, buddy."

"That's okay," Oliver reassured him earnestly, and Neil tousled the little boy's hair.

They looked awfully sweet together, and Maggie's heart did another round of somersaults. She glanced up to find Logan studying her.

"Uh-oh," he murmured. "I smell trouble."

She shot him a warning look. "Didn't Ruby tell you about Neil helping me with Oliver?"

"She told me, yeah. She also hinted that something else was brewing. I figured that was just wishful thinking, but looks like maybe she was right." He glanced toward the parking area and frowned. "Isn't he some kind of professor? Not exactly the kind of guy you usually get gooey over."

"He's a high school teacher, and I'm not—" Maggie stopped short. She'd been about to say she wasn't going *gooey* over anybody, but as of a few minutes ago, that wasn't technically true. And she never lied to Logan, not even about small things.

Never ever.

All of Ruby's HTPs had scars, and over the years, they'd learned to step carefully around each other's wounded places. Maggie's sensitive spot involved food.

Logan's had to do with the truth.

Dishonesty had destroyed Logan's childhood,

so as an adult, he was scrupulously truthful, and he demanded the same level of honesty from those closest to him. In his mind, there were no shades of gray when it came to lies, and he was better than a bloodhound at sniffing them out. Maggie had learned that the hard way, growing up, when she'd seen the hurt in her beloved brother's eyes over a little fib she'd told him. It had taken three months before she'd been back in his good graces.

She'd never made that mistake again.

So instead of protesting, Maggie went silent. Logan watched her closely for a minute, then sighed.

"You know about this guy's past?"

Maggie flashed him a warning look. "Logan, did you run some kind of police check on Neil?"

"Nope. Wouldn't be right to use the county's resources for personal business."

"Good."

"But I did call the sheriff's office in the town where he used to live and asked a few friendly questions, off the record."

"Logan!"

"You're my sister, Mags. This kind of stuff comes with my job description. Anyway, you can relax. The guy's clean as a whistle. He's carrying some baggage, though. It's bad, but it's not criminal. He hasn't talked to you about it?"

"No."

"And you haven't asked. Because if you did, then maybe he'd ask you some questions, too, huh?" Logan shook his head. "It's no good putting stuff like that off. If this has any possibility of going anywhere—"

"It doesn't."

"Come on, Mags. I saw some pretty intense sparks shooting around under that tent. You can't tell me you don't feel something for this guy."

"How I feel doesn't matter." When Logan snorted, Maggie lifted her chin and stared him down. "It *doesn't*. Oliver's adoption is my only priority right now, and I'm not going to run any risks of messing that up. I don't have room in my life at the moment for any…complications." She glanced toward the parking lot. The last thing she needed was for Neil to overhear this conversation. "Just drop it, okay?"

Her brother sighed. "I'm just trying to look out for you."

"And I appreciate it. But I'm not sixteen anymore, and I don't need your help managing my personal life."

"Maybe not, but from the look of that tent, I'd say you could still use a *little* help from me, sis. Tell you what. Put me some of those cookies in a bag, and I'll see if I can get this thing up for you."

"You've got yourself a deal."

* * *

Neil set the ice chest down to unlatch the gate to the dog park. He ushered Oliver through, pondering the complicated mechanics involved in shepherding a two-year-old through a busy parking lot. How did parents figure out this stuff every day? The last ten minutes had caused him more anxiety than writing his thesis.

Oliver bounced impatiently on the grass as Neil picked up the heavy cooler. The toddler caught his eye and grinned.

Neil grinned back. Okay, there were some pretty impressive perks, especially when the kid was as all-around great as Oliver.

The toddler had insisted on "helping" and was clutching a bottle of water in each hand. A playful breeze ruffled his hair, standing it on end. For today's excursion, Maggie had dressed him in denim shorty overalls with a blue-and-red-striped top. The bib of the overalls had a dog embroidered on it, and the socks peeking above the tiny tennis shoes sported paw prints.

Those details had Maggie written all over them. The woman loved a theme. He imagined her carefully coordinating Oliver's outfit for today while puppy-shaped cookies baked in the oven. And then getting up this morning and taking the time to stencil a little paw print on her own cheek.

It was a cute touch, but it wouldn't last the

day. After the tent had collapsed around them, when she'd been standing so close, he'd seen it was already starting to smudge at the edges. Of course, that was before she'd looked straight into his eyes. After that, everything had blurred and he'd been past noticing details. And when she'd stumbled against him under the fallen tent, when he'd reached out to steady her, for one moment, he'd come close to doing something profoundly foolish.

The truth was, if Maggie's brother had shown up about two seconds later, he'd have found Neil kissing his sister. Neil hadn't come that close to kissing a woman in a long while, and it had left him feeling unsettled.

And maybe a little disappointed.

Okay. A lot disappointed.

He had no idea what to do with that.

Back in the park, Neil set the cooler on the grass. Logan was fiddling with the metal tent supports and muttering under his breath. The sheriff made some mysterious adjustment, and the tent blossomed into its proper shape.

"Yay!" Maggie applauded. "You did it!"

Yeah, Neil thought wryly. *No thanks to me.*

Normally, his lack of manly mechanical abilities didn't bother him, but he couldn't help wishing he'd been the guy to put that smile on Maggie's face.

Logan stepped back to survey his work. "I'll tack it down so it won't blow away, and hopefully it won't fall on your heads. But get ready to order another one, Mags. This thing's a piece of junk. If it survives the day, I'll be surprised."

Neil went to examine the tent. "What was I doing wrong?"

"Nothing." The other man pointed to the center. "That hinge right there was bent funny, probably happened when they shipped it. I just straightened it, that's all."

Neil leaned forward to take a closer look. "I didn't notice that."

Logan studied Neil for a moment before speaking again. "Well, you've got to know what to look for. I've dealt with a lot of broken stuff in my time. I've gotten pretty good at spotting it. Not always so good at fixing it."

"Well, I'm glad you were able to fix this," Maggie interjected. "Today's going to be a scorcher."

Maggie sounded a little breathless, not at all like her usual buoyant self, and she was keeping her eyes carefully away from his.

Could be he wasn't the only one flustered by that almost-kiss a few minutes ago.

"Yeah, yeah." Logan pounded stakes through the holes in the bottom of a support, anchoring the tent into the grass. "Talk's cheap, Mags. I want my cookies. And don't be stingy. I didn't have time for breakfast." While Logan tacked down the second leg, Neil took care of the two on the opposite side of the tent.

When they were done, Logan strolled over to inspect Neil's work. It must have passed muster, because he left it alone and turned to his sister. "You got any more of those coolers out at the car?"

"Two more," Maggie said.

"I'll help Neil here haul them over, but then I've got to get back to the fundraising tent. The sheriff's department is in charge of the donations, and I've got the first shift." The radio clipped to his shoulder squawked. "Hang on a minute." Logan walked a few steps away and began speaking into the microphone.

"I don't think your brother has much faith in me," Neil said wryly when Logan was out of earshot.

Maggie was sorting cookies into a clear cellophane bag. "Don't mind Logan. He's always been tough on my—" She froze, one hand on a cookie—which, sure enough, was shaped like a puppy. "Don't pay any attention to him," she finished with a shaky laugh. "He's cranky. He skipped breakfast, and now he's manning a fundraising booth. Logan doesn't like asking people for money, not even for a good cause."

Neil had been a part of enough school fundraisers over the years to sympathize. Maybe he'd walk over in a few minutes and make a donation. He might not be able to put up a tent, but he could certainly drop a few bills for a good cause. Besides, it might do some reputation damage control with Logan.

Which, of course, shouldn't matter. There was absolutely no reason he and Maggie's brother had to get along.

Still. Neil reached for his wallet to check how much cash he had on him and froze when his hand encountered nothing but a flat back pocket.

"There!" Maggie tied the chubby bag of cookies with a curly blue ribbon. "These should sweeten up Logan's mood." She frowned. "You've got a funny look on your face. Seriously, don't let Logan get to you. He doesn't mean anything by it, honestly."

"It's not that."

"Then what's wrong?"

It took him a minute. The words were stuck in his throat. "I…uh…forgot my wallet."

He hadn't done that in years. He'd forgotten hundreds of other things—thousands, probably— but never…that. Not once. Not since…

But this morning, he'd been running late. He'd lost track of time grading some work Dex had sent in, and he hadn't wanted to keep Maggie and Oliver waiting. He'd been eager to get started, looking forward to the day ahead.

When was the last time he'd felt like that?

He didn't have to wonder. He knew.

The last time he'd forgotten his wallet.

"Oh." Maggie seemed puzzled. "Okay. Do you want to go back and get it? If you do, that's fine." She glanced at her watch. "We've got another half hour or so until they have the puppy parade. We're not supposed to start handing out the refreshments until after that. If you leave now, you should be back by then."

Just as Neil started to answer, his eye lit on Oliver. While the adults had been distracted, the little boy had opened the cookie tub. He had puppy-shaped cookies in each hand and icing smeared all over his face. From the generous litter of crumbs around his shoes, there was no telling how many he'd already devoured.

The kid was well on his way to making himself spectacularly sick.

"Oliver, whoa!" Neil stepped around Maggie and pried the cookies out of the child's fingers. "How many of these have you had?" Oliver set up a howl of protest, but Neil shook his head. "Sorry, buddy." He snapped the lid back on the tub. "No more cookies."

"Give me those." Maggie stood beside him, her

face tense. She held out her hands. "Give me the cookies," she repeated.

He stared at her, the missing wallet and all its implications forgotten. He'd never seen that expression on Maggie's face before.

She looked furious.

He handed the gnawed cookies to her wordlessly. She stooped to Oliver's eye level and handed one of the treats back to the wide-eyed child.

"You can have all the cookies you want, sweetie. But one at a time, okay? Start with this one, and I'll put the rest in a bag for you."

Without glancing at Neil, she snagged another plastic sack from the table, dropping the bitten cookies into it. She handed the baggie to Oliver.

"Here you go."

"Maggie." Maybe Neil didn't know much about kids, but even he knew that you didn't hand a two-year-old a bunch of cookies. "Don't you think maybe you should keep those for him and dole them out?"

She ignored him. "Oliver? I'm going to get you something to drink, okay?" Maggie unfolded a child-sized canvas chair and set it next to the toddler. "You sit here and eat your treat." She walked over to rummage in the ice chest, and Neil followed her, still bewildered.

She wouldn't look at him. She poured some

chilled water into a bright blue sippy cup, her mouth set in a tight, angry line.

"Maggie—" he started, and she turned to him, her green eyes icy hot.

"Don't ever do that again," she commanded in a low voice.

"What?"

"Don't ever take food away from my child again." She fumbled with the lid of the cup, her hands shaking violently.

As Neil watched her, his concern deepened. Something was very wrong here, but for the life of him, he couldn't figure out what.

"It was just *cookies*, Maggie. I was worried he was going to make himself sick."

"What's going on?" Logan walked over, his eyes cutting sharply between Neil and his white-lipped sister.

"Neil's leaving." Maggie handed Oliver his cup and snagged the overstuffed bag of cookies. She held them out to her brother. "Here you go, Logan. Thanks for fixing the tent." She turned back to Neil. "There's no point in your driving all the way back here today. Since Logan's here, he can unload the rest of the coolers and help me pack everything up after it's over."

He waited for a couple of breaths before speaking. "What about Oliver? Won't he be upset if I just…leave?"

Maggie didn't flinch. "I think he'll be fine. We've taken up an awful lot of your time lately. You're probably ready for a day off."

He didn't know how to answer this new Maggie with the hard eyes and the abrupt manner, so finally, he just nodded.

"All right. See you, Maggie. Bye, Oliver."

Oliver's lower lip started to quiver.

"Come on, Neil," Logan said. "I'll walk to the parking lot with you. I need to get the other coolers anyhow."

"Logan." Maggie's tone sounded like a warning.

Her brother ignored her. "The event's starting in about ten minutes, and that parking lot's going to get wild. If you want to get out, you'd better go now."

As they walked away, Neil heard Oliver whimper. He started to turn, but Logan clapped a firm arm on his shoulder, propelling him forward.

"Keep walking," Logan muttered. "Going back would only make things worse. She needs time to cool down."

"Clue me in. What just happened?"

"You stepped on a land mine."

"What?"

"Not your fault. You couldn't have known."

"I don't understand."

"Of course you don't." They'd reached the parking lot, and Logan halted on the sidewalk, weighing the keys in his hand. "But you will. If I know Maggie—and I do—before long she'll cool off and start feeling rotten. By this evening, she'll be ready to apologize. Unless I miss my guess, that's when she'll tell you."

Neil frowned. "Tell me what?"

"Nope." Logan shook his head. "This has to come from Maggie herself." The sheriff tilted his head and gave him a hard look. "I hear the kids over at the high school call you Iceman. That so?"

Neil met the other man's eyes squarely. "That's so."

"They have a good reason for that? Or is it just kids being kids?"

Neil waited a beat before answering. "They have a reason."

For a second, Logan looked taken aback. Then Neil saw a flicker of respect in the other man's eyes.

"You're honest. I'll give you that much. Well, do me a favor, Iceman. When my sister tells you her story, you listen good. And if you can't handle who Maggie is—all of who she is—then you back things up before you do any more damage than you already have."

Before Neil could come up with an answer, Logan strode away in the direction of the bakery van.

Chapter Ten

Late that afternoon, Maggie stepped over a sagging barbed wire fence and picked her way down the overgrown path leading to Sawyer's Knob. When she reached the overlook, she paused and surveyed the rapidly eroding area.

Ruby was right. The earth around the big hunk of granite was washing away at an alarming rate. Before long, there'd be nothing left but the slippery stone itself, jutting out over the ravine.

It was definitely time to put up a better fence. She'd have to mention it to her brothers.

She edged cautiously onto the rugged rock and peered down over the breathtaking view. Now, at the peak of summer, breezes rippled over the leafy treetops, and the smells wafting up were sweet and green.

In spite of its precariousness, there was something strangely peaceful about this high place where the hawks swooped and called right in front of your eyes. It always soothed her, and growing up, whenever Maggie had been feeling particularly bothered, she'd slipped away and come here.

Strange, because this was the only place that Ruby had ever cautioned her against.

It's a danger, Ruby had told all her kids. *That rock gets mighty slippery when it's wet, and the ground around it's crumbling away. You step wrong out there, you'll fall to your deaths, and you wouldn't be the first who'd done it, neither.*

Ruby's worries had been well-founded, and this place had only grown more dangerous over the years. Nowadays, even Maggie tended to avoid it, but she was on her way to apologize to Neil—and to explain what had happened at the park. She felt awful about the way she'd spoken to him, and she thought something she'd hidden here long years ago might help him to understand.

She wanted him to understand.

Picking up a long stick, she leaned over the rough gray rock ledge. The cleft she remembered was still there, its opening clogged with leaves. She gingerly cleared it with the stick, ready to bounce back fast if necessary. Once there'd been a skunk holed up in there, and today had already been bad enough.

Fortunately, nothing happened except that her stick clanked against metal. She dragged the old box toward the opening until she could pull it out. She dusted its top off gently. Then she sighed, picked it up and headed back down the brambly path.

Twilight was falling as she walked into the clearing where the old Sawyer cabin stood. She took a minute at the edge of the darkening yard to collect herself.

God, help me explain this, she prayed.

She squared her shoulders and walked up the stone steps to the porch. Lamplight shone from the living room windows. She raised a hand to knock, but Neil opened the door before she could, as if he'd been expecting her.

"Hi, Maggie." He looked down and frowned. "Oliver's not with you?"

"Not this time. He got so tired at the park that he zonked out on the ride home. He's been asleep ever since. He cried for a few minutes after you left, but then the dog parade started." Her mouth curved at the memory. "He was really excited. I definitely see a puppy in our future."

"I'm sorry I missed that."

Maggie drew in a breath. "I'm sorry, too, Neil. I shouldn't have bitten your head off. I'm sure you wondered why I did it."

He didn't answer, and as the silence stretched between them, Maggie remembered something Logan had told her. Sometimes the best way to get a suspect to talk was simply to go silent. Most people couldn't stand it, and they'd end up confessing. Now, as the quiet between herself and Neil grew heavier, Maggie understood why.

"I need to tell you something," she said. "And show you something, if you'll let me."

"Sure," he agreed readily. "Come on in."

Her fingers tightened on the box in her hands. "Could we talk out here on the porch?"

"Okay." He closed the door and motioned toward the large rockers in front of the living room window.

"I want to apologize," Maggie began as soon as she was settled.

"No." Neil spoke evenly. "I overstepped my boundaries. You're Oliver's parent, and I had no business—"

"No, it was me. I—" Maggie struggled, but the words wouldn't come. She handed him the box. "Here. I guess we should start with this."

He examined it in the faint light from the window. "A lunch box?"

"Ruby gave it to me not long after I came to Sweet Springs. No telling where it came from originally. Ruby saves things." Originally it had sported some 1960s-style flowers on it, but those had rusted and faded and were barely visible now. "Open it."

He set the container in his lap and flipped up the metal catch. He lifted the lid and took out the plastic baggie.

"It's full of old crackers." He looked at her, obviously puzzled. "I'm sorry, Maggie. I feel like I'm missing something here."

"That was my emergency box." When he still looked blank, she laughed wryly. "Sorry, it's kind of hard to explain."

"Take your time." Replacing the crackers, he closed the lid and put the box on the small table between them. He leaned back in the rocking chair, which creaked softly. At the noise, Rover scampered across the porch and jumped into his lap. Neil scratched the purring cat under the chin. "I'm not going anywhere."

Maggie unclenched her fingers and sighed. She looked out over the yard, grateful they were having this conversation on the porch. The small clearing was hedged by trees, lending it a sense of seclusion and safety. Inside it, everything was peaceful. Frogs sang shrill summer songs by the creek that trickled behind the cabin on its way down the mountain, and lightning bugs flashed yellow-green sparkles along the edge of the forest.

Up here, you felt separated from the world's troubles, and somehow, that made it easier to talk about them.

"I have this thing," she began quietly. "About food."

As they rocked together on the old porch, she told him about her childhood. She kept it simple, but there was no way to make it less ugly. She described going weeks without food, left alone in a ratty apartment by a single mother who was battling her own problems with addictions and mental health. She talked about eating dry pasta straight out of the box because she wasn't big enough to cook it for herself, and sobbing when she couldn't figure out how to work the can opener so that she could unseal a tin of pineapple she'd found.

"Of course, when I got old enough to go to kindergarten, there was free lunch and breakfast," she said. "That helped, but—"

"Whoa," Neil cut in sharply. "All that happened before you were *five*?"

She'd been watching the flickering lightning bugs, but something in his voice made her turn toward him. "Well, yes."

He stopped rocking his chair and stared at her, then nodded shortly. "Sorry. I interrupted you. Go on."

He sounded so grim that, for a second, she faltered. Still, she'd come too far to quit now. She might as well see it through. "It was a long time between lunch and the next day's breakfast, so I learned pretty quick to save food from my school meals to take home."

"Smart kid." Neil's tone was casual, but there was something not-so-casual thrumming beneath it.

"Not really. Because even after I got put into foster care, even when I got three regular meals a day, I kept saving food." She swallowed. "Having a stash of food made me feel safe, but it also caused a lot of problems. Foster moms didn't react well to finding spoiled food hidden in closets and dresser drawers, but I couldn't seem to stop. I got kicked out of one home after another. Until I came here, to Ruby."

"Ah." Neil put a lot of understanding in that one syllable. Maggie smiled at him. He was looking out over the moonlit yard, his face half turned away, but she knew he was smiling, too.

She could feel it.

"Ruby found my first hoard five days after I moved in. I'd stockpiled some cookies she'd given me in the back of my closet, and ants had gotten into them. She helped me clean it all up, and the whole time, I was waiting for the lecture." She darted a glance in Neil's direction and laughed half-heartedly. "It was always the same one, pretty much. The adults usually started off sympathetic. They'd reassure me that I had plenty to eat now, that I didn't have to worry. But by the second or third time they found food hidden in my room, they'd be aggravated. Finally, sooner or later, they'd call my social worker. I'd be removed from that home and taken to another one, and the whole process would start over."

"What did Ruby do?"

Neil, Maggie realized, was a good listener. In the past, when she'd shared snippets of her story, people had butted in to express outrage. Sometimes they'd ended up talking more about her past than she had.

"She gave me this." Maggie tapped the lid of the grubby box. "Then she took me to the supermarket, and we bought packs of crackers, my favorite kind. We stuffed the box so full it would barely close. Then she gave it to me to keep, and I took it out to Sawyer's Knob and hid it."

"Sawyer's Knob? The overlook?"

"That's right." Maggie smiled wryly. "Ruby wouldn't have approved of that part. It's not the safest place for a kid to go, but I'd found a little crack in the rock that nobody knew about but me."

Neil nodded slowly. "And that gave you a sense of control."

She nodded, relieved. He understood. "It wasn't just stashing the snacks. It was more the matter-of-fact way Ruby accepted that I needed them. Because, the truth is, it was never really about the food. It just came out that way. Comes out that way," she corrected herself ruefully. "Still. Like how I try to feed everybody who comes within ten feet of me. And my ridiculous meltdown today about you taking the cookies away from Oliver. I'm really sorry I flew off the handle."

Neil shook his head. "I'm the one who should be apologizing."

"Oh, but you didn't know—" Maggie started, but he interrupted her.

"Doesn't matter. I understand how it hurts when somebody hits a sore spot out of the blue like that. It's like stubbing a broken toe. You almost forget about it, but then you accidentally knock it against a piece of furniture, and it brings you to your knees. I'm sorry I caused you that kind of pain."

Maggie leaned closer and placed her hand on his arm, anxious for him to understand. "I didn't tell you all this to make you feel bad, Neil. You've been..." The right words danced just outside her reach, so she had to settle. "...great," she finished lamely. "So great with Oliver. So willing to help me, even though my problems have nothing to do with you. I felt terrible after you left. That's why I came up here and told you all this. So maybe you'd forgive me."

"There's nothing to forgive, Maggie. But thanks for trusting me enough to tell me."

"Thank you for listening." Their eyes met, and she was suddenly aware that her hand still rested on his arm. She flushed and removed it, tucking it back into her lap.

"I guess this is why you enjoy working in that bakery so much."

Maggie grinned. A job that required wearing an apron and a hairnet probably didn't sound very exciting to a brainy guy like Neil. "I do enjoy it. Being surrounded by food always makes me happy, and I absolutely love serving the customers. Whenever I put a plate in front of a hungry person, it's like I'm feeding that grubby little girl who was trying to make a meal out of uncooked noodles. I think I heal a little more with every dish I serve. The Lord works things out in amazing ways."

She'd never made that statement before in this church-rich region without hearing a quick and hearty amen. She waited for Neil to agree with her.

But he didn't. The only sounds were the rhythmic cheeping of the frogs behind the cabin and Rover's raspy purrs.

Neil shifted uncomfortably in his chair. Maggie's outspoken faith was nothing unusual. Here in Cedar Ridge, most people talked about God as if they'd just had lunch with Him. That never bothered Neil. He respected other people's beliefs, and he just kept his own doubts to himself.

And yet right now he felt as if someone had poked his heart with a sharp stick. Maggie had plenty of reasons of her own to feel betrayed by

God—but she'd salvaged her faith. Why hadn't he been able to?

After a couple of awkward seconds, she stood. "It's getting late. I guess I'd better be getting home."

Neil set Rover down on the porch floor and got to his feet. "It's getting dark. I'll drive you."

"No need for that. There's some moonlight, and I know the path like the back of my hand. Besides," she added with a smile, "the lightning bugs are putting on a show tonight. I wouldn't want to miss that."

He blinked. "Lightning bugs?"

"Well, yeah." Maggie lifted an eyebrow. "They're spectacular this time of year. Haven't you noticed?"

He looked out at the tree line. Yellow-green flashes flickered randomly here and there. Interesting, sure, but he wouldn't call them spectacular. Trust Maggie to see beauty even in bugs. "I haven't really paid much attention."

"Oh, but you don't know what you're missing! Come on." Maggie grabbed his hand, tugging him down the steps and across the yard. She stepped nimbly over the low wall where Oliver had taken his tumble and pulled him into the tree line.

"Now, close your eyes," she commanded.

"Why? I can't see fireflies with my eyes closed."

"Nobody calls them fireflies around here," she

chided. "They're lightning bugs. Shut your eyes and trust me."

He closed his eyes. As she led him forward, last year's pine needles crunched under his feet, and this summer's leaves brushed against his cheek. He probably should have been worried about stumbling over a stump and falling flat on his face, but he wasn't. His entire attention was focused on the feel of her slim, strong fingers closed around his own and the faint scent of cinnamon drifting from Maggie's hair.

It made him think of waking up to the smell of cinnamon rolls baking on a Sunday morning before church. Mostly when he remembered something happy, it brought a sharp-edged shadow of pain with it. This brought only a hungry longing—for peaceful mornings, cups of coffee and rich, sweet rolls shared in companionable silence. For a woman's head nestled against his shoulder, her red curls still tousled from sleep.

Neil's eyes flickered open, and he stopped walking.

Laura's hair had been brown, and she'd never liked to bake.

"You're peeking," Maggie accused him.

She stood just in front of him, the sliver of a moon silvering her ruddy hair and highlighting the sweet tilt of her nose.

"Look," Maggie whispered breathlessly. "Aren't they beautiful?"

Neil dragged his eyes from her face and tried to focus on the scene around them. The moonlit forest was alive with living sparkles, tiny lights darting all around them. "Yeah. It's hard to believe they're insects."

Maggie laughed. "That's what makes them so special. They're just bugs—and not very pretty ones if you see them in the daytime. But at night, when they're doing just what God made them to do, they turn into—" she gestured around them "—*this*! Don't you think that's amazing?"

I think you're amazing.

He didn't say the words aloud, but they echoed in his head just the same.

That anybody who'd been treated as badly as Maggie had been during her childhood could have such a strong desire to help others, to feed hungry people and to love an orphaned little boy who broke her heart at every opportunity…that was amazing, all right. And the fact that she was still so enthusiastic about simple things like cookies and fireflies?

To Neil, that was more than amazing. That was…

His brain fumbled for the right description and came up empty. He'd written more academic papers than he could count, and his vocabulary was off the charts, but he doubted there was any word in the dictionary that could sum up Maggie Byrne.

She chuckled. "There's one in your hair."

He reached up to flick it away, but she caught his hand.

"Careful," she whispered. "You don't want to squash him. Let me do it."

She tiptoed toward him, her eyes fixed on something just northwest of his forehead. He felt her hand gently brush against his hair.

The world closed in, just as it had when the tent had collapsed around them. Suddenly, nothing existed for him except Maggie. No past, no heartbreak, no guilt. Nothing but this beautiful, resilient woman who splashed on joy as if it were perfume.

For the first time in three long years, Neil's weary brain closed up shop and his heart woke up and took charge. As if it were completely natural, just as if it didn't mean that his entire world was tilting on its axis, he leaned down. He closed the scant inches between them until his mouth was only a breath away from Maggie's.

He paused for one questioning second as she looked up at him, her eyes wide and startled. Then, when she didn't pull away, he closed the gap.

And he kissed her.

He had forgotten what it was like, to lead with his heart without weighing the consequences. It felt good. After all the cold, lonely years, kissing Maggie felt like diving into tropical waters, so perfectly warm that you weren't sure where the air stopped and the sea started.

Maggie's hand slipped from his hair and settled lightly against his cheek. There was something about the innocent intimacy of that gesture that finally got through. He broke the kiss and stepped back.

She looked up at him, her eyes still wide.

"Wow," she murmured. "Iceman, my foot."

"I'm sorry." He didn't know what else to say.

"Are you?" Maggie sounded bewildered. "Then I probably should be, too. But I don't think I am."

"I was married." He blurted out the admission roughly.

"Oh." Maggie waited a second before prodding gently. "What happened?"

"She died three years ago. In a car accident."

"I see." That was all she said, but the two words were full of a quiet sympathy. She found his hand with hers and squeezed. "I'm so sorry, Neil."

"I haven't kissed anybody since…" He was making a disaster out of this. "I haven't been looking for—" He couldn't figure out how to finish that sentence.

He felt Maggie stiffen. "Don't worry about it, Neil. It was just a kiss. It doesn't have to mean anything."

She was trying to sound casual, but she didn't quite carry it off. The kiss had shaken her, too. Somehow, knowing that gave him the words he wanted to say.

"No," he argued quietly. "It meant something. I just...wasn't expecting it." A firefly flashed just beside Maggie's face, spotlighting her in its split-second glow. In spite of his confused emotions, Neil smiled. "You keep knocking me off balance, Maggie Byrne."

She'd turned her head to watch the firefly flit away, so he felt her answering smile more than he saw it. "Likewise," she said softly.

She gave his hand one last squeeze before re-leasing it. "I'd better get back home before Ruby starts worrying. Besides, you need to rest up. VBS starts bright and early Monday morning and lasts all week. I've volunteered us to help with the pre-school group."

Neil's brain was still on hiatus. All he could do was stare at her and think about how beautiful she was.

And how much he'd like to kiss her again.

"'VBS'?" he asked. "I've heard of it. What is it, exactly?"

She glanced up at him with a laugh. "You aren't from around here, are you? VBS is Vacation Bible School. It's a summer tradition for the churches around here. You and I are helping out at Cedar Ridge Christian. That's the church Ruby and I go to. Do you know where it is?" He managed a jerky nod, and she went on. "Great! Just meet me at the front entrance of the church at a quarter to ten Monday morning."

Bible school. Church. Neil's heart sagged like a deflated balloon.

"Maggie," he began.

She'd already taken a few steps down the path toward Ruby's farmhouse. She turned to smile over her shoulder at him, and his breath caught in his throat.

"Yes?"

I don't do church.

That was what he should have said.

Instead he said, "Be careful."

She nodded and waved. He watched her until she disappeared around the first turn of the winding path.

Neil sighed. The lightning bugs still swooped and sparkled around him, but all the beauty had gone out of the evening.

There was no way he was going to spend a week teaching preschoolers about a God he wanted nothing to do with. Sometime before Monday morning, he'd have to tell Maggie so.

And when he did, he had a feeling whatever that kiss had started would be over and done with.

Chapter Eleven

On Monday morning at 9:55 a.m., Maggie, Ruby and Oliver waited for Neil in front of Cedar Ridge Christian Church. The church's VBS was legendary, particularly the epic slip-and-slide that capped off the event every year, and the gray stone building buzzed with excited children.

This summer they'd chosen a jungle theme, and as usual, the decorating committee had gone all out. The entrance was festooned with leafy vines, and a pair of huge stuffed lions guarded the doorway. A recording of jungle noises played on a loop inside the foyer, and the cheerful volunteer handing out name tags sported a khaki vest and a safari hat.

"Your boyfriend's cutting things mighty close." Ruby glanced at her watch. "The kickoff starts in five minutes."

Boyfriend?

"Ruby, Neil's not—" Maggie protested, but then her mind skipped back to the kiss a few days ago. She stopped short, her cheeks tingling with color.

The truth was, she wasn't sure what her relationship with Neil was now—or even what she wanted it to be. Over the past couple of days, she'd gone through all sorts of feelings.

On the one hand, this—whatever it was—wasn't part of the plan. She'd made a firm commitment to steer clear of romance—at least until Oliver's adoption was finalized. And even then... Maggie intended for Oliver to have a stable family. The only kind of man she'd be interested in dating was somebody who was willing to commit long-term. Somebody capable of loving Oliver as his own, who looked on marriage as a no-matter-what, forever kind of deal.

Guys like that were as rare as unicorns these days, and Maggie certainly hadn't expected to stumble across one. And she still wasn't sure she had.

But she couldn't deny it—there was something special about Neil, something that had her hopes riding on a roller coaster. And ever since that heart-stopper of a kiss, she'd been wondering if maybe—

"Neil!" Oliver piped up excitedly. Sure enough, the red Jeep was pulling into the crowded parking lot. Maggie's nerves instantly started simmering like a sauce on a high heat.

"I'd better go save us some seats," Ruby said as Neil approached. "There's more folks than ever this year, and those pews are filling up fast." The older woman waved at Neil, then disappeared into the church.

As Oliver toddled toward his hero, Neil knelt and held out his arms. "Hi, buddy!" he said. Oliver grinned and hugged him tight.

Neil approached Maggie, Oliver beaming in his arms. As their eyes locked, all the everyday chaos surrounding them faded away. In a finger snap of time, she was back in the shadowy forest with sparkles of light dancing around them.

She could almost smell the pines.

"Hi, Maggie," he said, and her stomach flipped over. He glanced up at the gray stone building towering over them, and his expression shifted. "Listen—"

"In!" Oliver interrupted, pointing toward the open doors. "Go in!"

"He's excited about VBS," Maggie explained, studying Neil's face. One minute he'd looked so warm and friendly, and the next it was like he'd retreated somewhere inside himself and pulled down the blinds. "Neil? Is something wrong?"

He looked over at the decorated church again, then at Oliver. "I need to talk to you about something."

Drumbeats swelled from the sanctuary, followed by a burst of music from the VBS soundtrack.

The kickoff worship service was starting. The last stragglers on the sidewalk sprinted inside to take their seats.

"In!" Oliver wailed. "Pwease, Neil? Pwease?"

"Could we talk after the start-up session?" Maggie asked. "Oliver was beside himself when he saw all these jungle decorations. I know he doesn't want to miss anything."

Neil looked uneasy, but he nodded. "I guess so."

As she led the way through the short, tiled foyer into the soaring sanctuary, Maggie worried her bottom lip thoughtfully. What did Neil want to talk to her about? Whatever it was, it sure had him looking serious.

She wondered if it had anything to do with what he'd said right after he'd kissed her.

I was married.

Maggie tiptoed, finally spotting Ruby in the sea of singing people. Heading in that direction, she remembered the framed picture Ruby had discovered in the cabin and tried to imagine what sort of woman Neil's wife must have been.

A beautiful one, obviously. Probably a smart one, too. Somebody who'd been to college and whose bedside table sported a selection of literary masterpieces. Somebody who went to parties wearing a sparkly dress and high heels instead of an apron and sensible shoes. Who made witty conversation about art and current events, and who never sucked in her stomach when she passed a mirror.

The perfect woman. That was who Neil would've married.

Maggie, on the other hand, never wore heels without twisting her ankle, and the only sparkly thing she owned was a sequined chef's hat her brother Nick had given her as a joke. She'd never set foot on a college campus, and her bedside table held an assortment of vintage cookbooks purchased at yard sales, bristling with sticky notes.

No wonder Neil wanted to talk. She'd been so busy worrying about whether he might meet her criteria, she'd forgotten to wonder if she met his.

Sorry, Maggie, but I've thought it over, and you're not really my type.

They ducked into the pew beside Ruby, who gave Maggie a sly look as she scooted over to make room. The song ended, and the congregation rustled onto their seats as the pastor stepped to the podium.

"Welcome," Pastor Thompson said, "to our jungle!" When the applause died down, he continued, "This theme isn't as far-fetched as it seems. The truth is, sooner or later, every Christian finds himself lost in a jungle of some kind—a dark place that tests his courage and his faith. The trick is not to set up camp there, so this week we'll learn how to find our way through the jungles in our lives—by following God."

Another round of enthusiastic applause broke out. Neil shifted in his seat, and Maggie glanced at him. He wasn't clapping. A muscle jumped in his jaw, and his expression was unreadable.

"God loves us, and He'll never leave us to struggle through the jungle alone. He—"

"That does it," Neil muttered. He gently settled Oliver in Maggie's lap and got to his feet. "I have to go." He strode toward the exit.

Maggie stared after him until Ruby elbowed her sharply in the ribs. "Ouch!"

"Don't just sit there." The older woman scooped Oliver off Maggie's lap and plopped him in her own. "Go after him."

"But—"

"I'll look after Oliver. Here, baby." Ruby pulled a tiny stuffed lion from her purse. "Look what Grandma Ruby has." She wiggled the toy in front of the squirming toddler.

Oliver was instantly smitten. "Kitty!"

Ruby chuckled. "Close enough. Hurry up, Maggie, before you miss your chance." When Maggie hesitated, she added, "Honey, this ain't the time to dither. *Go talk to him.*"

Maggie frowned. Something about Neil's abrupt departure had Ruby concerned, and her foster mom's instincts were usually right on target. Maggie jumped up without further argument.

Neil was almost to his Jeep by the time she caught up to him. He had his keys in his hand and a grim look on his face.

"Neil!"

He turned, his expression changing to wary resignation.

"Sorry, Maggie, but I can't do this. I'm not a… religious person. I haven't set foot inside a church since my wife's funeral." He glanced at the steeple towering over them. "Not until today."

"Oh." Maggie wasn't sure how to respond to that, and in any case, this wasn't a conversation to have in the middle of a parking lot. Her eye lit on the gate leading into the church's prayer garden. She grabbed Neil's hand. "Come with me."

She tugged him into the small courtyard. At this hour, the little square of green lay in the church's shadow and the air was pleasantly cool. Maggie dropped onto a damp concrete bench and motioned for him to do the same. "Now we can talk."

Neil didn't answer. He seemed distracted by a weathered stone cross set among lush ferns. An engraved plaque bore a partial verse, My Peace I Give unto You.

"Neil?" Maggie prodded gently.

He sighed. "I told you my wife—her name was Laura—was killed in a car accident."

"Yes."

"She was bringing me my wallet. I'd left it at home." He shook his head. "That was nothing new. You know me, always forgetting stuff. Laura had the day off—she was an RN—so I called and asked her to drop the wallet by the school. She just laughed and said sure." His throat flexed. "It was the last time I spoke to her."

"That's… It must have been terrible."

"More terrible than you know. Laura was eight months pregnant. That's why she'd taken the day off work, because she had an ultrasound appointment. I was supposed to go with her." His hands clenched into fists. "I begged off at the last minute. I'd been with her to all the other ones, and my school was doing standardized testing that day. I knew my students wouldn't focus as well with a substitute, and I was worried about their scores. Laura was fine with it. It was a routine appointment, and the technician was a friend of hers. She'd promised to bring me a video of the ultrasound."

He paused, and Maggie braced herself. Whatever had happened, Neil needed to gather his strength to talk about it.

"When she started to turn into the faculty parking lot, a student T-boned her. The kid was running late for the test, so he was speeding…and texting. He slammed into the driver's side, never even hit the brakes. He was banged up pretty badly, but he made it. Laura didn't. I heard the sirens from my classroom, but I had no idea…" He went silent, and Maggie heard her heartbeat pounding frantically in her ears. "The kids wanted to look out the windows, but we were about to start the test, and I didn't want them distracted. I closed the blinds and told them to sit down. When my coworkers realized who was in the car, my principal came running for me, but it was too late." He cleared his throat. "They said she lived for a few minutes. If I'd looked out the window, seen the car, maybe… But I didn't. I knew Laura was driving to the school, but it never crossed my mind…" He cleared his throat again, roughly. "The whole thing was my fault."

"Oh, Neil, no." She laid her hand on his wrist and squeezed. "That's heartbreaking. But it wasn't your fault."

He lifted his chin and met her eyes. "The kid was texting *me*, Maggie. He was late to my class, and he was messaging me to let me know. Back then, I gave my students my cell number, and they messaged me all the time. My principal didn't approve, but I had a tendency to bend the rules, and I hadn't paid much attention to his objections. So, yeah, it was my fault. But not only mine." He glanced back at the cross with a fierceness that made her pulse jump. "A hundred things had to line up for the accident to be as serious as it was. So many lives—Laura's, our baby's, mine, my student's—were balanced on a knife blade that morning. If God had shifted the timing by a few seconds, everything could have been different. When I realized that, I was done with God. I haven't been to church since."

Maggie's brain and heart struggled to catch up. She'd seen the pain in Neil's eyes the day they'd met, but she'd had no idea how deep his wounds actually were. They cut not just to the bone, but to the soul.

"I'm so sorry," she whispered. She was. Her heart broke for Neil's pain—and a little bit, self-ishly, for her own. The fragile dreams she'd been secretly spinning disintegrated like cotton candy in the rain.

That was that. Neil Hamilton wasn't for her. It was surprising how much that realization hurt, but the pain didn't change anything.

During her childhood, Maggie had known too many people who answered to nobody but themselves, and she'd seen up close how easy it was for them to twist the truth to justify their own views and vices. Because of that, she'd decided years ago that the only man she could trust with her heart was one who'd already entrusted his own heart to God. Now that she had Oliver to consider, that was more important than ever.

She didn't know quite how she'd missed this. She should have…checked. She should have asked. But none of that mattered now.

She cleared her throat. "Thank you for telling me, Neil. I really… I needed to know this."

He nodded and stood. "I'm still happy to help you with Oliver, just not at church. I've changed a lot since Laura's death—mostly in ways I'm not too proud of. But I've never been a hypocrite, and I won't start now. Not even for Oliver." *Not even for you.*

He didn't say the last words aloud, but he might as well have. She rose to her feet.

"I wouldn't ask you to."

Neil scanned her face. "This bothers you."

"Of course it does. Not the VBS part. Like I said, I wouldn't ask you to do anything you weren't comfortable with. But…what you went through, Neil, losing your wife and baby like that. I'm just so sorry. And then losing your faith, too. That must've made everything even harder." She swallowed. Better to get everything out in the open now. She lifted her chin and looked him in the eye. "My faith is really important to me."

His eyes searched hers. "How important, Maggie?"

She understood what he was asking. She sighed, but there was no way around it. "Very."

"I see." He nodded, but there was so much regret in his eyes that her heart constricted painfully. "I guess we'll leave it there, then. I'm sorry, Maggie. I wish things could've been different."

He meant it. She heard the sincerity in his voice, and somehow, that made it hurt even worse. She suddenly understood even better what Neil had said—about how everything could've been different, how his pain and joy had been balanced on a knife blade that had tipped the wrong way. Right now she felt as if she'd just gone running up the dock only to see her cruise ship sailing away, with banners flying in the wind, leaving her behind.

Maggie sighed. "I wish things could've been different, too."

They looked at each other for a moment. Then Neil nodded shortly.

"You'll need to get back to Oliver. I'd better go."

"Hold your horses."

Neil and Maggie turned. Ruby stood framed in the courtyard's gate, holding Oliver's hand.

* * *

Neil glanced at Maggie. She was frowning at her foster mom, who frowned right back.

"Ruby, Neil's explained everything. He's not comfortable—"

Ruby waved away her words with an age-spotted hand. "I reckon the man can speak for himself. This shindig's getting started, and Oliver has to go to his class. You take him, Maggie, whilst Neil and me get this straightened out." The older woman leaned down, tipping the toddler's chin up. "Mrs. Vivien's teaching your Bible lesson today, baby, and guess what she told me? Every boy and girl in her class gets a surprise to take home!"

Oliver looked uncertain—but interested. "Surprise?"

"That's right. So you'd better go in with Maggie lickety-split, before they're all gone."

"Bye-bye, Neil. Maggie! In!" Oliver waggled his fingers desperately, asking to be picked up.

Neil knew Maggie couldn't—and shouldn't—resist that plea. She shot a concerned look in his direction as she hurried to Oliver, hoisting him up into her arms.

"Ruby—" she started, but the older woman shooed her away.

"Go on. There's lots of kids here today, and I'd

hate for Vivien to run out of flashlights before Oliver gets one."

"Fwashwight?" Oliver's eyes lit up, and Neil noticed that the little boy dropped his *l*'s, a sure sign he was excited.

Ruby grimaced. "Kind of let the cat out of the bag, didn't I? Well, try to act surprised or Vivien will have my hide. Now, get, the both of you."

Oliver pointed toward the church. "Go, Maggie! Pwease?"

"All right, sweetie. We're going." Maggie left the garden, throwing one last worried glance over her shoulder before she disappeared around the corner.

Ruby dropped onto the bench with a soft grunt. "Damp," she pronounced disapprovingly. "Going to make my arthritis flare up, sure as the world, so let's get right to it. What's this trouble between you and the good Lord?"

Nope. Not a conversation he wanted to have. "Mrs. Sawyer, with all due respect—"

"Save your breath," the older woman interrupted with a shake of her head. "No point telling me to mind my own business. I've never been much good at that. Now, I only caught the tail end of what you was telling Maggie. Tell me the whole of it, and don't leave nothing out. Then you let me say my piece, and you can go on home if you're still bound to it. And we won't talk about it no more unless you bring it up your own self. Do we have a deal?"

Neil started to refuse, but then he thought... why not? Once she heard how he felt, Ruby would likely back away from him just like Maggie had done. Might as well get it over with.

"Fine." He dropped down on the bench across from hers. "I'll tell you, if you want to know."

And he did.

Ruby Sawyer, it turned out, was easy to talk to. Her expression shifted as the story went on, but nothing seemed to shock her. There was a kindly shrewdness in her eyes, and she nodded here and there. Somehow, without saying a word, she made him feel like she was on his side.

When he'd finished, she cocked her head like an inquisitive sparrow, studying him. "That all of it?"

"Yes."

"Good," she said with a satisfied nod. "You ain't near as far gone as I feared you were. No," she said when he tried to interrupt, "I heard every word you said. You believe in God, all right. You've just been real mad at Him for the past three years."

She made him sound like a petulant two-year-old. "I don't think you understand—"

"Course I understand. I seen it lots of times." Ruby shifted on the bench and grimaced. "With every single one of my kids. The clever ones, now, those are the hardest. Take my Ryder. Smart as a whip, that boy, so he took the longest to come round. Stands to reason you're going to have a real tough time."

He wasn't following. "With what?"

"Trust, mostly," Ruby replied simply. "And fear. You can dress it up with your three-dollar words if you want to, but that's what it boils down to. You're mad because God allowed something that hurt you real bad, and you're scared to trust Him again. Like I said, it ain't nothing I ain't seen before. Some of my young'uns...you wouldn't hardly believe me if I told you what they lived through before they found their way to my house. They had lots of reasons not to trust folks—nor God, neither."

Neil recalled what Maggie had told him about her childhood. "I'd believe you."

"Well, then, maybe you'll believe me when I tell you what comes next. You got to decide if you're gonna trust again or not. In your case, that means believing God knows what He's doing." She leaned forward, holding his eyes with her own. "Even when things don't make no sense to you, even when you can figure four or five different ways you think He coulda done things different. Even when it hurts worse than anything you've ever felt before." She shrugged. "For a smart fellow like you, that's hard 'cause you're so used to trusting your own thinking." She chuckled wryly. "For an old lady like me, now, it's a sight easier."

He studied the plainspoken woman. "I think you're a very smart old lady, Ruby Sawyer."

She patted him briskly on one arm. "Well, good, 'cause this smart old lady doesn't see why Vacation Bible School has to be a problem for you. I know," she said, when Neil started to speak. "I take your point, and I don't like hypocrites any better than you do. But look here. Nobody's asking *you* to teach a lesson nor lead a prayer nor nothing like that, are they?"

Neil opened his mouth to argue, then shut it.

No. They weren't.

Ruby flashed a smug smile. "See? You can keep right on thinking all the stinky thoughts about God you want to. Won't nobody know the difference. All you got to do is sit through some preschool Bible lessons, for Oliver's sake. That's all VBS amounts to—well, that and some snacks and a few arts and crafts. You ain't scared of that, surely, a smart man like you?" When Neil didn't answer, she heaved herself to her feet. "Well, you think it over, and do what you will. I've said my piece, and I'm supposed to be helping out in the kitchen. Just remember, now, a flashlight from the dollar store's only going to keep that boy happy for so long. He's getting better, but he still relies on you a good bit. Maggie, too. And if you ask me, both of 'em have had enough disappointments for one lifetime without adding any more."

Thinking hard, he watched the elderly woman walk slowly away.

What she'd said made a lot of sense.

Maybe he was overreacting to the church thing the same way he'd been overreacting to that kiss he and Maggie had shared. For the past few days, he hadn't been able to think of anything else. He hadn't felt so much as a flicker of interest in another woman since Laura, so this whole thing with Maggie had blindsided him.

He'd been doing his best to figure it out, to cope with the feelings she was dredging up. To complicate matters, last night he'd had an email informing him the curriculum-development job in Virginia was his if he wanted it.

A week ago, he'd have accepted in a flash. Instead he'd asked for a few days to think it over, because of Maggie and Oliver and the unexpected possibilities that had begun tickling around the edges of his mind.

He should've known better than to hope, but he had, a little. Until he'd seen that unmistakable look on Maggie's face a few minutes ago.

Now he had a choice. He could go home and spend the evening nursing his disappointment and socializing with a cat. Or he could take Ruby's advice, go inside and try to finish what he'd started. He could spend his last few weeks in Cedar Ridge trying to help two people he'd come to care about.

He glanced back at the steeple and came to a decision. He'd go in and suffer through Vacation Bible School. Ruby was right. No cutesy preschool lesson was going to make any difference to Neil's opinions, and Oliver would be happier if he was there. That was all that really mattered.

Cedar Ridge Christian was a large, thriving church, and Neil had to ask directions twice before he found Oliver's room. The whole preschool area had been transformed into a jungle extravaganza. Artificial plants were clustered in the corners, decorated with bright paper flowers. Stuffed monkeys dangled from crepe paper vines looped around the ceiling. A plump, gray-haired woman sat on a beanbag chair in front of the room, facing a group of small children. The kids were sitting cross-legged, all holding flashlights and shoeboxes.

"All right, everybody," the teacher was saying as Neil slipped in to join Oliver and Maggie. "Switch on your flashlights!"

Maggie looked at him and lifted her eyebrows. He smiled sheepishly and shrugged. She smiled cautiously back.

Oliver had been absorbed in switching on his

blue flashlight, but when he noticed Neil, he grinned happily. "Wight?" he called, waving to the teacher. "Wight for Neil?"

"That's okay, buddy," Neil said quickly. "I'll share your light."

Oliver looked at his flashlight lovingly, then at Neil. "Okay," he agreed after a long second. "We share."

"Wonderful, Oliver." The teacher gave him an approving smile. "Now, does everybody have their lights on? Good! Put the flashlight in the box and close the lid."

The children obeyed with soft thumps and rustles.

"Can we see the light now, children?"

A negative murmur. No, they couldn't see the light anymore.

"Is it still on?" the teacher asked.

There was a difference of opinion. Some of the children said no. If they couldn't see the light, it must not be on. Others, like Dex's brother, Rory, maintained that the light was on inside the box.

Neil watched Oliver closely, but the little boy didn't commit either way. He just watched the teacher warily, clutching his precious box with both hands.

"Let's see!" the teacher suggested. "Lift the lid just a little and peep inside." There were happy noises as the children discovered their flashlights still burning.

"God's love for us is a little bit like this. It lights up our lives," the teacher explained. "Sometimes we forget about Him, and that's like putting a flashlight in a box. Then we can't see the light, but that doesn't change God. He still loves us just the same, doesn't He?" She nodded solemnly, and all the preschoolers followed suit.

Except for Oliver. He was still peering into his box, looking at the cheap flashlight faithfully burning. Something about the awed expression on the child's face made a lump rise in Neil's throat.

Maybe he didn't share this faith anymore, but still, if church brought comfort and joy to people like Oliver and Maggie, then it was worthy of Neil's respect, if nothing else. There was far too little comfort and joy in this world to quibble over where it came from.

Oliver must have felt Neil's gaze, because he held the opened shoebox over for him to peek into.

"See, Neil?" the child murmured, his voice soft with wonder. "See? Owiver gots God. In a *box*."

That did it. All the feelings prickling in Neil's throat snorted out in a laugh. Maggie, Oliver and the teacher all shot him concerned looks, but he couldn't help it. He tried. He covered his mouth in an effort to stop the noise, but it didn't do much good. He laughed until tears streaked down his face.

Vacation Bible School might not be so bad after all.

Chapter Twelve

The following Friday, Cedar Ridge Christian Church was gearing up to celebrate the end of its best-attended VBS ever. After a fabulous and exhausting week, all the volunteers and participants were looking forward to the long-anticipated finale—the legendary slip-and-slide.

Maggie studied the scene with a rising sense of panic. There was a good reason the slip-and-slide that capped off each VBS was considered epic. The church perched on a hill, and every year, volunteers smoothed a straight path down the steepest part, removing all the rocks and debris. Then they unrolled an incredible length of heavy yellow plastic and turned on the hoses, creating a homemade water slide that even adults found thrilling.

Maggie had done her share of sliding since coming to Cedar Ridge, and it had always been her favorite part of VBS. But when she thought

about Oliver going down that massive thing…
Well. That was another matter altogether.

She bit her lip and slanted an uncertain glance at Neil. "Does that look safe to you?"

He stood beside her, Oliver in his arms, looking worried. "Are you kidding me? A little kid's supposed to go down *that*?"

Oddly, Neil's concern made Maggie feel better. She wasn't being overprotective after all.

"Ah, a scared first-time mommy." Vivien, the preschool teacher, paused to give Maggie's arm an understanding pat. "I can always spot 'em. Don't you worry. All the little folks have to go down with an adult. We haven't had any injuries yet."

"Okay." That information probably should have made her feel better than it did.

A teenage boy was first down the slide, yelling gleefully. When he hit the bottom, a huge wave of pooled water splashed up and the crowd cheered.

Oliver cheered, too. "Swide!" He pointed urgently to the line of kids waiting their turn. "Swide!"

"All right." Maggie took a shaky breath. "Miss Vivien says we go together, Oliver. I'm not sure how exactly, but I guess somebody will show us. Come on, and we'll get in line."

"Wait." Neil shot her an embarrassed look. "Would it be okay if I went down with him first?"

Maggie had held out her arms, but she dropped

them to her sides with a sense of relief. She hadn't felt any too confident about her ability to hold on to Oliver, but Neil surely could. "You don't mind? You're not wearing trunks. You'll get soaked."

"I don't care." He paused. "Do you?"

She shook her head. No, she didn't. For the first time, she was actually happy to let Neil take over. "Go ahead."

"Here." He pulled off his glasses and handed them to her. "Hang on to these, will you?"

"Sure."

"Thanks." His unguarded eyes met hers, and Maggie's heart stuttered. Seeing Neil without his glasses for the first time felt strange. Sort of... personal.

She watched as the two of them went to join the line. Oliver bounced excitedly in Neil's arms, talking up a storm. He must have said something funny, because Neil rumpled his hair and laughed.

Maggie's lips curved. They looked so comfortable together. They easily could have been taken for a father and son.

Her smile started to fade, but she jerked up her chin and refused to let it. Today was a happy day. They'd had a wonderful week, and it was silly to spoil it by wishing for something more.

Oliver was doing much better. Although he still preferred Neil, he turned to Maggie more and more. Neil tried to encourage that, always giving her a chance to provide what Oliver needed instead of jumping in to do it himself.

That strategy was paying off. Just today, Oliver had been working on a craft involving a paper monkey with movable arms and legs, and he'd needed help opening the brads that fastened the pieces together. For the first time ever, he hadn't even asked Neil. He'd gone right to Maggie. After she'd opened the metal pieces for him, she and Neil had shared big, goofy grins and a surreptitious fist bump.

That was about all they'd shared since their talk in the prayer garden—smiles over Oliver's progress and polite conversation. Maggie wasn't sure what Ruby had said to make Neil change his mind about VBS. Ruby wouldn't say. Whatever it was, it obviously hadn't changed anything else. Neil behaved as if their kiss had never happened.

Which, given Neil's disappointing stance on faith, was a good thing, Maggie reminded herself firmly. She couldn't afford to mess things up—especially right now. Mrs. Darnell had been well pleased with Oliver's progress at her last home visit.

"He's not there yet," she'd said, "but he's much closer than he was. You're officially licensed for foster care now, so we can formally transfer Oliver from Ruby's care to yours. And if things keep

moving in this direction, I'll feel confident rec-
ommending the adoption."

That was exactly what Maggie had been praying for. She should've been over the moon with
joy. And she was.

Mostly.

It was just that sometimes, when she remembered that kiss, she had a feeling she'd missed out
on something awfully special. She'd been trying
not to think too much about it, but the feeling
lingered heavily underneath her happiness about
Oliver's progress.

"You're not going down?"

Startled, Maggie turned to find Logan standing beside her, dressed in his uniform.

"In a minute, maybe. I'm doing the nervous-
mommy bit first." She pointed to Neil and Oliver, who were now almost to the front of the line.
"You're up-to-date on all your first-aid training,
right?"

"Yeah, but I think you're good." Logan narrowed his eyes as Neil and Oliver settled at the top
of the slip-and-slide. "I may not know much about
that guy, but I read people well enough to tell you
one thing. He'll protect that kid or die trying."

Maggie blinked. There was a grudging admi-
ration in her brother's tone, and Logan handed
that out sparingly.

Looking back at the top of the hill, she saw

Neil's muscles tense as he wrapped his arms around Oliver's small body.

Logan was right, she realized, her gaze fastening on Neil's determined expression. Oliver was safe in his care. As the two of them pushed off, Maggie relaxed and her mouth actually tipped into a genuine smile.

They whizzed past, and she heard their voices mingled in a shout. "Whoooaaaaaaaaaaaaaa!"

Maggie laughed. Boy, how the two of them loved that silly word. Oliver said it constantly now. It nearly drove her bananas, because every time he said it, it reminded her of Neil.

Suddenly, the disappointment she'd been trying so hard to ignore for the past several days took a sudden stab at her heart, and her laughter broke into silly, snuffling tears.

"Told you," Logan said as a huge plume of water crested over Neil and Oliver at the base of the slide. "They made it fine. They're— Hold on. Are you *crying*?"

Maggie waved him off. "I'm fine."

Her brother leaned in close, his face creased with concern. Then, "Hamilton!" he boomed.

Neil was walking up the hill, soaking wet, a dripping Oliver chortling in his arms. At Logan's shout, he broke into a jog.

"Everything okay?" he asked as he neared them. He looked at Maggie and frowned. "What's wrong?"

"You tell me," Logan said. "Any particular reason my sister should burst into tears when she looks at you?"

"Logan!" Maggie said, feeling her cheeks redden.

"Swide," Oliver said, pointing urgently toward the line at the top of the hill. "Again, Neil. Again."

"Okay, buddy. Just a minute. Maggie, are you sure you're all right?"

"I'm fine." She glared at Logan. "It's just nerves. Somebody needs to mind his own business."

"Sorry, Mags." Her brother shook his head. "Boyfriend or not, a guy makes you cry, he becomes my business."

She froze as her eyes and Neil's connected. "Logan, Neil and I aren't…" She trailed off, trying to think of the right way to say it.

"Maggie and I aren't together." Neil said it for her.

"Oh." Logan looked from one to the other. "From what Ruby said, I thought—" He stopped short. For once in his life, he didn't seem sure what to say.

"Down!" Oliver demanded irritably.

"Okay, bud. Hold your horses." Neil set the toddler down on the grass.

"Oh." Maggie suddenly remembered the glasses she held in her hand. She held them out. "Here."

"Thanks." Neil settled them on his nose and blinked at her, his expression worried. "Good thing I got you to hang on to them for me. Going down that thing's like jumping into a pool." As he spoke, he shoved his hands into his pockets. "Uh-oh." His expression changed to horror.

"What is it?"

"I forgot about my phone." He pulled a dripping cell phone out of his pocket.

"Oh, man." Logan leaned in, looking at the device. His face was sympathetic, but Maggie had a hunch that her brother was as grateful as she was for the distraction. "It got soaked, all right. Is it still working?"

"I'm not sure."

"Neil! Swide! Pwease?"

"Sure, buddy," Neil said. "Hold on just a second, okay?"

"Now!"

Neil pressed a button, and the screen lit up. "It still works," he muttered. "But maybe I should—"

"Owiver swide," the toddler announced impatiently.

"I'll take you—" Before Maggie could finish the sentence, Oliver darted away from them, stepping onto the slick yellow plastic.

Her heart jammed in her throat. "Oliver, wait!"

He halted in the center of the slide just as a

teenage boy launched himself from the top of the hill.

Neil was the first to react. He dropped his phone and lunged forward, Logan and Maggie right behind him. None of them were quick enough.

The teen did his best to put on the brakes, but there was nothing he could do. He slammed into Oliver at full speed, knocking the little boy sideways.

Neil dropped to his knees beside Oliver. The toddler lay flat on his back at the bottom of the slide, perfectly, terribly still.

"I'm so sorry!" The dripping teenager hovered nearby, his face pale. "Is he okay?"

"Oliver!" For one awful second, Neil's heart stopped. Then Oliver jerked upright, sucked in a breath and began to yell at the top of his lungs.

"Good sign," Logan muttered. "When they can howl like that, I always feel better." He checked the little boy over with careful fingers. "I don't think anything's broken, but that was a pretty hard knock. Probably should run him over to the emergency room just to be on the safe side. You carry him up to the parking lot, Hamilton, and I'll bring my car around."

"Come here, buddy." Neil moved to scoop up

Oliver, but the sobbing child looked past him and held out his arms entreatingly.

"Maggie! Maggie!"

"I'm here, sweetie. I'm right here." She knelt and gathered the toddler into her arms. "It's all right. Uncle Logan's going to take us to the doctor in his car with the flashy lights. Won't that be fun?"

Neil cupped a hand under Maggie's elbow and helped her struggle to her feet, Oliver nestled against her chest. "I'll meet you at the hospital."

Maggie looked at him, her eyes stricken. "Thank you." The short whoop of a siren summoned her, and she stumbled toward the parking lot.

As Neil watched her go, the weight of what had just happened settled heavily over him. Why had he been worried about his phone? He should have been holding Oliver's hand. If he'd been paying attention, like he should have been, this wouldn't have happened.

"Here." Ruby appeared at his elbow, offering a beach towel. "Wrap up so you don't drip all over the waiting room. I'd go myself, but they don't need all of us, and I got a feeling Maggie'd rather have you. Tell her I'll be praying up a storm. Now, go on." She gave him a firm push. "Get. She'll feel heaps better once you're there with her."

Would she really? He wasn't sure, but if she

would, then he'd be there. He nodded shortly. "I'll call you and tell you what the doctor says."

"You do that." Ruby patted his arm.

As he jogged toward his Jeep, someone called behind him. "Iceman! Wait up!" Dex hurried in his direction, carrying Rory in his arms.

"Dex, I'm sorry. I can't talk right now. I've got to go—"

"Yeah, yeah, I know. Here." The teen held out Neil's phone. "You forgot this. I thought you might need it over at the hospital."

"Thanks." He accepted the phone with a wince.

"That's all right." The boy clapped him on the arm and gave him a man-to-man look. "Kids, bruh. They'll scare you to death sometimes. Tell Maggie not to worry, though. We'll all be praying for Oliver." For once, there was no suspicion or reserve in Dex's face, only a sympathetic concern that Neil found touching.

"I'll tell her."

"God's got this," the boy said with a nod. "Tell her that, too. Tell her I said so."

"I will."

As Neil drove to the small local hospital, his brain weighed his guilty concern over Oliver against Dex's words.

God's got this.

Dex had sounded so sure, and like Maggie, he'd seen plenty of tough times.

As Neil waited out Cedar Ridge's lone traffic light, he cleared his throat awkwardly. "God," he said aloud, trying it out. "You know how I feel about You, but if it'll do any good, You can add my prayers for Oliver in with the rest of them. Please, just let him be all right."

He found Logan pacing the emergency waiting room, talking on his radio. He glanced up when Neil entered.

"They already took him back."

"Can I see them?"

"Sure. That'd be okay, wouldn't it, Donna?"

The blonde nurse behind the counter shook her head without looking away from her computer screen. "No visitors in the back, Logan. You know the rules."

"Make an exception. This guy's my sister's—" Logan gave Neil an uncertain look "—good friend," he finished finally. "The boy's really attached to him."

The nurse glanced up and sighed. "Oh, all right. If the sheriff vouches for you, I guess that's good enough for me." She nodded toward the door to her left. "Exam room three."

Just as he reached the door, a doctor came out. Neil's gaze shot over the man's shoulder and zeroed in on Maggie's face, trying to read her expression.

She looked relieved. Everything must be okay.

Neil's tense muscles relaxed so fast that he had to brace himself against the frame.

"He's fine," Maggie announced cheerfully. "No broken bones, just some bruises. We're waiting on some paperwork, and then we can go home."

"That's great news," Neil said. Oliver, snugly wrapped in a striped hospital blanket, was cuddled in Maggie's arms. He looked up sleepily as Neil leaned closer. "Hiya, buddy."

"Neil." Oliver yawned. The toddler nestled closer to Maggie and closed his eyes with a little sigh.

"They gave him a children's pain reliever." Maggie stroked Oliver's hair. She glanced at Neil, and he read her thoughts—as clearly as if she'd spoken aloud.

See how he's letting me hold him? Isn't this wonderful?

Neil straightened and stuck his hands in his damp pockets, feeling suddenly awkward.

Ruby was wrong. Maggie didn't need him after all.

And neither did Oliver. Not anymore. But there was still something Neil needed to say.

"Maggie, I'm really sorry. I should have been holding his hand instead of focusing on my phone."

"What are you talking about?" She frowned up at him. "You think this is your fault?" She shook her head. "Neil, it isn't. I'm the one that yelled at him to stop right when he was in the middle of the slide. Sometimes accidents just happen, no matter how careful we try to be."

"All right." A different nurse bustled in, brandishing a clipboard. "We just need Mom's signature. Hi," she said to Neil with a smile. "You must be Dad."

There was a short, uncomfortable pause. "No," Maggie said finally. "Neil's a friend."

"Oh! Well, then, I'm sorry. Only family's allowed back here."

"But—" she started. Neil cut in quickly.

"I should go home anyhow, get dried off. I'm really glad Oliver's going to be okay."

"He is," Maggie whispered, dropping a kiss on the top of the toddler's head. "He really is going to be okay now." She was talking about more than the accident, Neil realized.

"Yes," he agreed quietly. "I believe he is."

They made such a sweet picture that Neil lingered for a second, trying to press the image deep enough into his memory so he wouldn't forget. Maggie, her ruddy curls pulled away from her face, summer freckles dotting the bridge of her nose. Oliver, swathed in a striped blanket, cuddled close in her protective embrace. They looked like what they were: a mother and child. A family.

Just the two of them.

Clearing her throat, the nurse tapped the pen on the clipboard. "Bye, now," she said with a bright firmness.

Maggie looked up, her eyes shining. "Thank you, Neil," she said softly. "For everything."

For everything. Neil understood what that meant. Maggie wasn't only thanking him for stopping by to check on Oliver. She was thanking him for *everything*.

She was telling him his job was done.

"You're very welcome," he answered quietly.

He left the exam room, striding past the waiting area, not pausing when Logan called his name. He went to the parking lot, climbed into his Jeep and drove straight to the cabin. Rover greeted him at the door, but Neil's dampness discouraged feline friendliness, and the cat soon stalked off.

Rover had a point. Neil's clothes felt clammy and unpleasant, and he needed a long, hot shower. But first, he powered up the computer. As he waited for the email program to open, he told himself that everything had worked out for the best.

Maggie and Oliver didn't need him now, and that was a good thing. He appreciated Maggie's kindness today, but the truth was, he didn't have the best track record for looking after people he cared about. That was something he couldn't afford to forget.

The email interface was up and ready. Neil scrolled to the appropriate message and hit Reply.

Thank you, he typed as Rover watched him disapprovingly from the bedroom doorway. I'll take the job.

Chapter Thirteen

Sunday evening, Neil lingered in the church foyer as a familiar drum-heavy kids' song swelled from the crowded sanctuary. He wasn't sure he wanted to go in. In fact, he'd debated coming at all.

Tonight was the special service spotlighting the Vacation Bible School participants and volunteers. There was no real reason for him to be here, and at least a couple of good reasons to stay home. He hadn't heard from Maggie since Oliver's accident, and the weather service was forecasting a nasty storm.

In the end, he hadn't been able to stay away. He'd arrived a few minutes late because he hadn't wanted to make small talk. He only wanted…

He wasn't sure what he wanted.

Just that, whatever it was, it was here.

He scrutinized the packed room. With the jungle decorations removed, this sanctuary resembled a hundred others. It had the standard arched, stained glass windows and oak pews, the simple wooden cross on the wall behind the pulpit, the usual high, vaulted ceiling. It even had the obligatory, churchy smell of lemon furniture polish, spicy carnations and candle wax.

This place was nothing special. Yet, for the past two days, he'd missed coming here.

He'd expected to miss Maggie and Oliver. That was a given, but he hadn't expected to miss *church*.

It made no sense. Nothing special had happened here. He'd sat through Bible stories and songs geared for the not-quite-potty-trained crowd. He'd passed out carefully cut-up food on tiny plates— all provided by Angelo's, of course—and then thrown 90 percent of those snacks in the trash. He'd helped with so many messy crafts that he'd be finding glitter on himself for weeks. He'd gotten a crick in his neck listening to long-winded, lisping prayers with frequent mentions of both pets and cartoon characters.

If anything, he should feel relieved it was over. He didn't. But he should.

The theme song ended, and the pastor thanked the volunteers and announced a slideshow. The sanctuary lights dimmed, and different music began to play. Candid snapshots flashed one by one on the big screen at the front of the church.

Neil watched intently, picking himself, Oliver and Maggie out in various photos. There was that first flashlight activity—the one about how God was faithful all the time, even when you couldn't see Him. The following photo was taken the day they'd searched for the lost monkey—a lesson about how God came looking for those who lost their way. Neil smiled. Oliver had been brimming with joy over the red stuffed monkey he'd been given to take home. And there they were in the kitchen, everybody sporting orange construction-paper manes. They'd decorated lion-shaped cookies to remind them that with God on their side, they could be brave. Maggie had been in her element that day, and she'd glowed when Oliver had chosen *her* to help him stick licorice whiskers on his lion.

And there… Neil stared at the glowing screen. Actually, he had no idea what activity they were doing in that picture. He was holding Oliver, and the little boy was laughing. Neil was grinning, and Maggie was looking at them both, love shining in her eyes.

Love for *Oliver*, he reminded himself.

The slideshow clicked ahead, but Neil's mind stayed fixed on the image he'd just seen. As he pondered that sweetly affectionate look on Maggie's face, he came face-to-face with the truth he'd been ducking for the past several days.

He wanted her to look at him like that. More than anything.

Somewhere along the way, he'd fallen for Maggie. He'd never expected to feel this way about a woman again, but there was no doubt about it. In fact, he knew it with a certainty that floored him.

Not that it mattered. Because when he'd admitted how he felt about God, all he'd seen in Maggie's eyes had been disappointment—and pity.

As the slideshow ended, thunder boomed and the sanctuary lights flickered ominously.

The pastor chuckled as he reclaimed the podium. "Looks like we finished up just in time! Let's give our VBS volunteers a big round of applause and head downstairs to the fellowship hall for refreshments."

After a hearty spate of hand clapping, people surged up the aisles. Neil saw Maggie weaving through the crowd, leading Oliver by the hand. She'd embraced the safari theme with her usual enthusiasm. Two ponytails tied with jute tumbled over her shoulders, and she'd paired a leaf-sprinkled green top with khaki cargo shorts. Oliver's red shirt sported a big orange lion.

"Hey, Iceman," Dex called. Neil pulled his gaze away from Maggie to see the teen hurrying toward him. Rory was balanced on his brother's muscled arm, wearing his paper lion's mane. "Did you grade my exam?"

"I did. It was a solid B, so you're eligible to play ball." He smiled. "Congratulations."

Dex's face lit up. "You hear that, Rory? Your big brother's one good season from getting a ticket to play college ball. Thanks, man. I 'preciate your help, and I'm sorry I gave you a hard time to start with." The young man looked uncomfortable. "You know, about Maggie and all. I had it wrong. When Oliver got hurt, I could see you really cared about both of them. Anyway, I owe you big for this. Anything. Anytime. I mean it, Iceman."

Neil managed a smile. "Send me a ball cap from whatever college team recruits you and drop the Iceman thing, and we'll call it even."

"I'll send you the cap, all right." Dex offered Neil a fist bump and a wink. "But you're always gonna be Iceman. Sorry. That name's stuck."

"Great," Neil said dryly.

"Yeah," the boy answered seriously. "It could be, if you wanted it to. Your name's what you make it, and I think you got a lot of *great* in you, Iceman." The boy grinned. "Ain't nobody more surprised about that than me. Now, come on, Rory—let's grab us some cookies and celebrate!"

Neil watched Dex go, feeling a sense of subdued satisfaction. At least he'd helped one Cedar Ridge student. Not a great count for the years he'd spent here, maybe. But better than nothing, and he was glad he was ending his teaching career on a positive note.

"Neil!" Maggie stepped out of the chattering flow of people to stand beside him. "You came. I wasn't sure—" She stopped herself. "I'm so glad. Look who's here, Oliver."

The little boy didn't release Maggie's hand, but he reached for Neil's with his free one. "Neil! Whoa!"

His throat threatened to close as small, familiar fingers twined around his. "Whoa, buddy. Good to see you." He glanced at Maggie. "He's all right? No problems after the accident?"

"Nothing but a couple of bruises. We're very thankful." She offered a tentative smile. "And we have some wonderful news. Mrs. Darnell approved the adoption. After the paperwork makes its way through the system, we'll have a finalization ceremony at the courthouse. Then we'll be a family forever. Right, Oliver?"

"Forever family," the toddler repeated carefully. "Maggie and Owiver." He looked up hopefully. "And Neil?"

"No, honey." Her voice wobbled. "Remember? Forever family is Maggie and Oliver. Neil's our good friend. Our very, *very* good friend."

Oliver pushed out his lower lip. "Neil, too!"

"Well, he'll come to the ceremony, sweetie. Won't you? It would mean so much to him." Maggie searched Neil's eyes with hers. "It would mean a lot to both of us. This might never have happened without your help."

He cleared his throat. "I'd love to. The thing is… I'm moving at the end of the month. I've turned in my resignation to Audrey, and I was just about to give Ruby notice on the cabin rental. I took a job in Virginia."

"Oh." Maggie's hopeful smile drooped. "Virginia. A teaching job?"

"Curriculum development."

"I see," Maggie whispered.

The minister approached, gently herding the last of his congregation down the aisle. As he stepped into the foyer, he snapped off the lights. The sanctuary plunged into darkness behind him, except for the lightning flickering through the stained glass.

"Time for cookies." The pastor smiled at Maggie. "Word is Angelo's sent over a batch of spectacular ones, all shaped like jungle animals."

In spite of the heaviness in his chest, Neil smiled. He knew who'd made those cookies, and it definitely wasn't Angelo.

"We're headed that way now," Maggie said. "Aren't we, Neil?"

He wanted to say yes. He wanted to sit with her and Oliver and eat cookies and drink fruit punch and pretend for a while longer that things were different. That the three of them were really what they'd appeared to be in the slideshow. A family.

But they weren't, and he might as well face that fact now.

"I'd better get back to the cabin. I have a lot of packing to do." He gently disentangled his fingers from Oliver's and rumpled the little boy's hair. "See you later, buddy."

"See you, Neil," Maggie answered for the both of them.

Oliver's lip trembled, and as Maggie led him in the direction of the stairs, he looked wistfully over his shoulder at Neil. But he never let go of her hand.

As they edged out of sight, Neil sighed and glanced again at the sanctuary. Lightning flickered, briefly highlighting the stained glass windows.

"Well," he murmured under his breath, "if You were going to answer somebody's prayers, I'm glad You decided to answer Maggie's. That's something, I guess. In fact, that's a lot. So…thank You."

He waited for a second, then chuckled, slipping one hand beneath his glasses to rub wearily at his eyes. What was he still standing here for? If he'd learned anything over the past three years, it was that his conversations with God tended to be very one-sided.

As Neil turned toward the doors, something in the darkened sanctuary caught his eye. He squinted, then took off his glasses. He wiped them on his shirttail, put them back on and squinted again.

Strange. A thin beam of light was shining upward from one of the pews.

Neil's heartbeat sped up, and he blinked, annoyed with himself.

Oh, for crying out loud. You know there's got to be some reasonable explanation, Hamilton. Go see what it is.

He strode down the carpeted aisle. Just as he'd expected, it was nothing. Just a flashlight, one of the cheap plastic ones the teacher had passed out the first day of VBS. Some child had turned it on and left it behind, wedged between the cushion and the wooden back of one of the middle pews.

See? Perfectly simple explanation.

But as Neil picked it up, the words the preschool teacher had said murmured in his memory.

God's love for us lights up our lives. Sometimes we forget about Him…but that doesn't change God. He still loves us just the same.

Neil looked up at the shadowed wooden cross hanging on the back wall of the church. For a second—just for a second—he wondered.

Then he shook his head, disgusted. He was being ridiculous. This was a flashlight from the dollar store. It didn't mean anything, except that some poor kid was just as forgetful as he was.

He switched it off and tossed it back into the pew.

He made it halfway up the aisle, then stopped and stood there in the dark church for a few long seconds, his back to the altar, breathing in the smoky scent of spent candles. The silence filled his ears like cotton.

Then he turned and retraced his steps to pick up the forgotten toy. He lingered there for a few moments, weighing it thoughtfully in his hand.

When he walked out into the muggy air of a Georgia June evening, the hilt of a blue plastic flashlight stuck out of his pocket.

Back at the farmhouse, Maggie helped Ruby wash the last of the dishes as the predicted thunderstorm brewed outside the kitchen window. When the rain started in earnest, Ruby shook her head.

"We're in for a gully washer, sure as the world. Half the Knob's liable to be down in the hollow by sunrise."

Maggie nodded absently as she dried a saucer. The weather was the least of her concerns. "I'd better check on Oliver before I head to bed. He might get scared if the thunder gets too loud."

She sighed. "Poor little fellow. He cried himself to sleep. He's so upset about Neil moving away."

"How are you feeling about that yourself?" Ruby pulled the plug, allowing the sudsy dishwater to swirl down the drain.

Loaded question. Seeing Neil at the church had been…hard. And hearing he was moving away had been even worse. Still. Maggie struggled to keep her expression neutral. "All things considered, I expect it's for the best. Don't you?"

"No, I don't!" Ruby wrung out her washcloth with a fierce twist. "I think it's a shame. Watching you two together all week got my hopes up, so I'm real disappointed to hear Neil's leaving town. But I ain't done yet. I'm going to keep right on praying over this until the good Lord slams this door in my face." Ruby nodded firmly. "You never can tell how God will work things out. Ain't nothing impossible for Him."

Maggie sighed. Ruby and her matchmaking. "I thought you'd have given up on that idea."

"Why? Because Neil's faith is in a tangle? No, that never worried me so much." Ruby sat down at the table and patted the chair beside her invitingly. "I sorta took it as a testimony to how close Neil and God really are, deep down. You know how it is. We always get the maddest at the ones we love the most. Besides, I think that's near about over anyhow. Neil stuck out the week at church all right, didn't he?"

Maggie nodded as she sat at the table. "Yes, he did." And most of the time, he'd seemed to be enjoying himself.

"And by the end of it, I could tell the Lord was working on him." Ruby chuckled. "Ain't that funny? Smart man like that, all those fancy degrees, and a little old Vacation Bible School turns him around. The baby class, no less! God sure does have a sense of humor, don't He?"

Maggie frowned. Come to think of it, Neil had seemed awfully attentive to the lessons, and she'd even seen him talking to Pastor Thompson a couple of times in the hallway. "I think you might be right, Ruby. I hope so."

"I know I'm right. I feel it in my bones. But you still ain't going to try to talk him out of moving to Virginia?"

"No, I'm not. And don't you try it, either," she added hastily. Ruby was perfectly capable of it.

"I can't promise anything. Like I said, I'm still praying and believing that God's got a better plan in store for you two," Ruby retorted. "Go ahead and give me all the side-eye you want to, but that man is made and meant for you, and you for him."

Maggie laughed humorlessly. "I don't see how you could think that. We're as different as night and day. You saw that box full of degrees and awards he has." She stopped and swallowed. "And the woman in the picture must have been his wife, Laura. She wasn't just beautiful. She was a nurse." Maggie shook her head. "I don't see any way Neil and I could work out, not long-term, and I have Oliver to consider."

"Ah." Ruby nodded sagely. "So *that's* what this is all about. I been wondering, 'cause you're generally not the kind who gives up on folks easy. You're worried you ain't good enough for Neil, and you're scared to death he'll figure that out for himself and turn his back on you after you've learned to love him. So you're putting up all kinds of walls, just like little Oliver did, trying to stave off the heartache."

She leaned back in her chair and sighed. "I'd hoped maybe the good Lord and I had loved that fear out of you over the years, but I guess maybe it's something like this old hip of mine. Does fine most of the time, but it still flares up now and then, and always at the worst possible moment."

She reached across the table and gathered Maggie's hands in hers. "But you can't listen to fear, Maggie, my love. Listen to old Ruby, instead. Some of the best blessings we ever get are on the other side of what we're most scared of. Love's always a risk, that's for sure. But it's the risk most worth taking, child, and life would be mighty empty without it."

Lightning flashed blindingly outside the window, and thunder boomed, shuddering the walls of the old farmhouse.

"Now, that one was a mite too close." Ruby released Maggie's hands and rubbed her arms uneasily. "Got me prickling all over."

"I'd better check on Oliver." Maggie rose, relieved at the change of topic. "That's sure to have woken him up."

As she hurried down the short hallway, she pondered what Ruby had said. Her foster mom was right. Now that she thought about it, there *had* been signs this past week that Neil's stance against religion was softening, lots of them. Maggie didn't know why she hadn't noticed that herself—unless Ruby was right about the rest of it, too.

Could it be that Maggie had given up on Neil so quickly because her own childhood fears were reasserting themselves? Was she behaving like Oliver had, pushing away somebody she was starting to care about because she was afraid she'd get hurt?

If so, that wasn't a good thing. Maggie knew the damage fear could do all too well.

When she reached Oliver's bedroom, she frowned. The door was open much wider than she'd left it. She stepped into the small room, warmly lit by the glow of a night-light.

"Sweetie?" The bedcovers on the toddler bed were tossed back, and there was no sign of Oliver.

Maggie snapped on the overhead light and scanned the room. It was empty. Stepping back through the doorway, she glanced down to the end of the hall. Just as she'd feared, Ruby had propped the back door open to allow cool air to flow into the old house. Only the lightweight screen door was closed, and that would be easy for a child to push open.

Please let it be latched. If it is, I'll know Oliver is still in the house. But if it isn't...

Maggie hurried to test it, and the flimsy door swung wide. The hook-and-eye latch hadn't been fastened.

Her heart lodged in her throat, Maggie stepped onto the back porch, slick from the blowing rain.

"Oliver?" She heard nothing over the roar of the wind and the sound of raindrops pelting the tin roof. "Sweetie, answer me!"

Lightning flashed again, giving her a clear glimpse of the path leading to Neil's cabin. Oliver had cried for Neil before going to sleep. She'd thought she'd settled him down, but maybe she hadn't. She fumbled frantically in her pocket for her phone.

He answered on the second ring. "Maggie? What's wrong?"

"Oliver's missing! I think he's headed up to the cabin. He was so upset about you moving away—"

"He's not here," Neil cut in, sounding alarmed. "If he'd shown up, I'd have called you."

Of course he would have. Maggie's heart sank. "He might still be on the path. I don't know how long he's been gone. Neil, I'm worried. This storm is only getting worse."

"We'll find him." She heard a frantic rustling. "I'm getting my shoes on now. You search the yard and check the barns. He can't have gotten far in this weather. I'll look around the cabin, and then I'll head down the trail."

"Neil—" She heard the plea in her own voice. He answered it swiftly.

"It's going to be all right. We'll find him. I promise."

"All right." She knew, of course, that there was no guarantee he could keep that vow, but somehow just hearing it steadied her nerves. She remembered what Logan had said about Neil, back at the church. *He'll protect that kid or die trying.* "I'll search the barns."

"If you find him, let me know. I'll be heading your way." The call disconnected.

"Maggie?" Ruby called softly from the kitchen doorway. "What on earth's going on?"

Maggie tried to get a handle on herself before

she answered. She shouldn't upset Ruby any more than she had to. "Oliver's not in his bed. I think maybe he slipped off to the cabin, but don't worry. I've already called Neil, and he's going to help us—"

"Maggie, that child hasn't gone anywhere. He's sound asleep in your bed, this very minute."

"He's what?" Maggie ran up the hallway and stumbled into her room. Sure enough, there was Oliver, spread-eagled on her bed. His stuffed VBS lion and monkey were snuggled under one arm, and he was holding her nightshirt against his face.

"He probably got upset, what with the storm and all that talk about Neil leaving town," Ruby murmured, "so he just climbed into his mama's bed, where he felt the safest. Most natural thing in the world for a child to do. Come on." She slipped one arm around Maggie's waist. "If you're bound to cry, at least do it in the kitchen. No sense waking the boy up."

Back in the bright kitchen, Maggie rubbed weakly at her eyes. "Ruby, that scared me half to death."

The older woman chuckled. "Welcome to motherhood, honey. Take a few deep breaths. All's well that ends well."

"Oh!" Maggie gasped as a belated realization struck her. "I've got to tell Neil. Maybe I can catch him before he gets far from the cabin." She punched in his number with shaky fingers.

"You sure called him mighty quick, I notice. Before you even told me or searched the house."

Maggie shot her foster mom a glance. Ruby's eyes were twinkling. "I wasn't thinking straight." She frowned as Neil's voice-mail recording picked up. "He's not answering. He probably forgot to take his phone with him. He was going to search around the cabin and then start this way."

"Then he ought to show up on our doorstep shortly, and we'll give him the good news. I'll make a nice pot of hot cocoa. That's just what a body needs after being out in a rainstorm like this. It's a real doozy." Ruby moved toward the stove and began gathering her ingredients, shaking her head. "No telling how much of Sawyer's Knob will be gone by tomorrow. The whole of it's likely to have crumbled away."

"The Knob." Maggie's blood chilled. "Neil doesn't know we've found Oliver, and I've talked to him about the Knob. There's no way he'll come all the way here without checking there first."

Ruby's face paled. "It ain't safe," she whispered. "Especially not in a storm like this. If somebody don't know it well—"

"Stay with Oliver. I'm going to find Neil." Snatching up a rain jacket, Maggie barreled out into the hammering rain.

Chapter Fourteen

Halfway down the trail, Neil switched the flash-light into his other hand and reached for his phone to see if he'd missed a call from Maggie. There'd been no sign of Oliver around the cabin, and Neil was hoping the toddler had turned up in one of Ruby's barns.

His shirt pocket was empty. He must've left his phone back at the cabin. Frustrated with himself, Neil batted away a dripping branch so force-fully that it whipped back and slapped his cheek. Served him right. Thanks to his stupid absent-mindedness, now there was no way Maggie could let him know if Oliver had been found.

Well, there was nothing he could do about it now, so maybe he should look on the bright side. For all he knew, Maggie had already called with the good news that Oliver was safe and sound.

Neil hoped so. This storm was too wild for an

adult to be out in, much less a toddler. The rain poured down in sheets, making the red clay trail dangerously slick, and the lashing wind was turning sticks and pine cones into projectiles.

On the positive side, the cheap flashlight he'd brought home from church had turned out to be a lifesaver. Its little beam fought the darkness as Neil stumbled along, yelling Oliver's name into the roar of the storm.

There was no answer.

Please, God. Please. Keep him safe. Help me find him.

That desperate prayer had been repeating in the back of Neil's brain for some time before he realized it. And when he did realize it, he didn't stop. It was as if his long-buried faith had gone through some kind of emergency reboot, bypassing all his anger and all his questions.

After he'd gotten back from the church, he'd set the little flashlight on the table, determined to sort out his confused feelings about God and think things through logically. Then Maggie had called with the news about Oliver, and logical thinking had flown out the window.

Right now, in the teeth of this storm, there was no room for doubt. Tonight, he simply needed all the things the VBS teachers had talked about to be true. He needed God to show up and get them through this.

Neil paused to wipe his rain-splattered glasses on his shirt, but it didn't help much. Lightning flashed, quick, successive flashes, followed by a rolling, shuddering crack of thunder that reverberated against his chest.

"Oliver!" Neil called again, but his voice was swallowed by the hammering of the rain.

He's probably fine, he reassured himself. *I'll get to the farmhouse, and Maggie will tell me they found him.*

If not… Neil's heart flinched away from the worst possibility, from the agony it would cause Maggie—and him—if anything had happened to Oliver.

He knew the kind of pain you risked when you loved as Maggie did, without limits. Wasn't that why he'd shut himself off after Laura's death? Easier to be alone, to wrap himself up in his grief like a ratty old blanket, refusing to care about his students, his friends. Himself.

In the end, he'd turned into such a coward that he'd been reluctant to care about a stray cat.

But then Oliver had shown up in his yard, with Maggie following behind him. Maggie with her cookies and her generous smiles and her habit of seeing the best in people. She'd sneaked up on his blind side and found her way into a part of his heart he thought he'd blocked off forever.

Somehow, sometime over the past few weeks,

he'd fallen in love with her, with both of them. It was as simple—and as complicated—as that.

That was why he was determined to figure out his faith, why a child's forgotten flashlight had stopped him in his tracks tonight. Because of Maggie and Oliver, because Neil wanted desperately to believe that maybe he'd accepted that Virginia job a little too soon. That maybe it was time to crack open the shoebox he'd stuffed God in after the accident.

But then this had happened, and until they found Oliver, nothing else mattered.

He was over halfway to the farmhouse now, and he'd seen no sign of Oliver. That was good. Probably meant the little boy hadn't come this way at all. Just as Neil breathed a sigh of cautious relief, the flashlight's beam lit on the old marker Maggie had pointed out to him on their first trip down this path.

Sawyer's Knob.

Neil frowned. He'd forgotten about that place. He'd been to the overlook only once after Maggie had told him about it. It was an impressive view, but the eroding ground was alarmingly unstable. He hadn't been back.

Surely Oliver wouldn't have ventured that way. He'd have stuck to the path, just as he had the day he'd shown up at the cabin. Neil was almost sure of it.

Almost sure, but not completely. He needed to check it out.

Following the flashlight's beam, Neil thrashed down the overgrown path leading to the Knob. Wet brambles snagged at his pants—and reassured him. It was unlikely a toddler could have made it through here.

As he neared the Knob, dangling leaves brushed against his face, reminding him of the crepe paper vines of VBS. He glanced down at the flashlight in his hand.

Look, Neil! I gots God.

In spite of his worry, Neil smiled at the memory. Then the little beam found the Knob—or what was left of it—and his smile faded.

It was almost completely gone. The pointed granite rock remained, but now it jutted into empty space. The surrounding earth had liquefied into a mudslide, pouring sloppily down into the valley below.

He didn't think there was any way a small child could have made it up the overgrown trail, but Oliver had surprised them before. Neil needed to be absolutely sure.

Holding his breath, he picked his way toward the slippery rock, rivulets of water rushing over his shoes. Under the flashlight's shaky beam, another couple of inches of ground crumbled away, and the prayer repeating in the back of his brain increased in volume.

Please, God. Please.

Neil leaned over the edge, straining his eyes against the darkness. As his balance shifted, he slipped, and for a heart-catching second, he slid forward. At the last minute, his fingers found a crack in the rock, and he scrabbled for a handhold.

Once he'd steadied himself, he aimed the light down the slope. It didn't do much good. The flashlight beam wasn't strong enough to reach the bottom of the drop-off.

If Oliver had fallen down there, Neil needed to know. Somehow, he'd get to him. He didn't know how, but somehow, he'd find a way. The problem was, he couldn't *see*.

"God!" Neil muttered aloud in desperation. "Please!"

He wasn't sure what he expected to happen, and nothing really did. The storm raged on unchecked, and the lightning flashed, brilliantly illuminating the valley for one precious split second. Neil scanned the slope in that instant, looking hard.

No Oliver—at least, he didn't think so. If he could get another look—

As if on cue, the lightning flashed again, several quick flashes in a row. Thunder cracked and rolled above him. The storm was directly overhead, and the rain was coming down harder than ever.

But none of that mattered. The lightning had given him a clear view of the whole drop-off, and there was no child crumpled at the bottom of it.

Thank You. As he turned to pick his way back up the trail, his heart awash with relief, the prayer refrain changed. *Thank You, God. Thank You.*

"Neil!" Maggie's frantic shout reached him just as he stepped back onto the main path.

Lightning flickered, giving him one quick glimpse of her running in his direction before she launched herself at him. He staggered backward, and the flashlight spun into a puddle as his arms went around her waist.

She was shaking like a leaf. "I'm so sorry," she murmured into the hollow of his throat. "I didn't check the house before I called you. Turns out Oliver hadn't gone anywhere. He—"

"Whoa." With some reluctance, he pulled away, peering under her rain hood into her face. It was too dim for him to read her expression. "Oliver's okay? He's safe?"

Her head bobbed. "He was in my bed the whole time. I didn't even think to look there. I tried calling you—"

"I forgot my phone."

"I figured, so I tore out here as quick as I could.

Ruby and I were scared you'd head out to the Knob. I'm so glad you didn't!"

"I did. Most of it's gone over the edge, by the way. I nearly slid over myself."

"Oh, Neil." Maggie's whole body shuddered. "You could've been killed, and it would have been my fault." She put her arms back around his waist, hugging him so tightly that the breath whooshed out of him.

They were getting soaked standing out here in the downpour, but Neil didn't care. He put his arms around her slippery raincoat and held her close.

She smelled like vanilla tonight, like everything good and warm and wholesome. He breathed the scent in gratefully, and then he spoke into the gap between her hood and her hair.

"No," he told her. "It wouldn't have been your fault if I'd fallen, Maggie. It wouldn't have been anybody's fault. Sometimes things just…happen."

People, well-meaning people, had told him that over and over after the accident. He hadn't really believed them, but now he knew it was true. He knew it all the way to the toes of his waterlogged shoes. A weight lifted from his heart, and joy, pure joy, rushed in like the torrent of water he'd seen rushing over the Knob. Relentless and unstoppable.

He lifted his hands to frame her face, cupping her head through the slick plastic hood. He couldn't see well, but he didn't need to. He closed his eyes, leaned in and found her lips on the first try.

When he lifted his mouth from hers, her sigh puffed against his chilled cheek.

"Whoa," she whispered.

"Whoa," he agreed softly. "I didn't fall. Oliver's safe. Everything's all right."

She touched his cheek, her fingers slick with rain. "God is good," she murmured. He knew it was a question, and he gave her the answer she was waiting for.

"Yes, Maggie." *All the time. Even when we can't see it clearly, when we don't understand.* "God is good."

"Maggie!" A male voice called from the direction of the house, and the beam of a strong flashlight sliced through the rain.

"Coming," she shouted back at the top of her lungs. "We're both coming." She turned to Neil. "That's Logan. Ruby must've called him as soon as I left. We'd better get back, or he's likely to have half the sheriff's department looking for us."

"Hold on a second." Neil leaned over and scooped the plastic flashlight out of the puddle. He stuck it carefully in his jacket pocket, then put one arm around Maggie, drawing her close. "All right. Now I'm ready. Let's go home."

* * *

Twenty minutes later, Maggie and Neil stood arm in arm in the doorway to her room. They watched Oliver, still peacefully asleep. Lightning flickered outside the bedroom window, but the rumbling thunder was much fainter. The storm was ebbing.

"So, he was here the whole time?" Neil asked ruefully.

"Apparently," Maggie admitted. "He's never come to my room during a storm before. I figured he'd slipped away again, and I panicked and called you." She reached up and smoothed back a wet lock of his hair. Ruby had stripped them of their raincoats and thrown huge towels at them, but they were still dripping wet. Maggie knew she probably looked like a drowned rat, but she didn't care. Oliver was safe, and Neil's arm was around her, holding her close. Nothing else mattered. "I'm sorry for worrying you—and getting you soaked."

"Don't be. I'd rather be soaked and worried with you than safe and dry at home alone."

What a sweet thing to say. Maggie's eyes filled. "Same," she whispered. She touched his face, feeling the roughness of his unshaven cheek against her palm. "That's why I was so quick to call you tonight. I knew you'd do whatever it took to help me find Oliver, but I also just wanted…needed… you here with me."

He tipped up her chin so that their gazes met fully. "I hope you mean that, because I don't think the job in Virginia is going to pan out. I think— I hope—God's still got some work for me to do right here in Cedar Ridge."

"You're going to keep teaching?" She smiled up at him. "Really?"

Neil laughed. "Exactly. I'll be *really teaching* this time, not just going through the motions. I'm pretty sure once I explain that to Audrey, she'll be willing to tear up that resignation I sent her. But that's not all." He paused. "The truth is, I was wondering if there might be a couple openings in that forever family you're putting together."

Her heart tripped on a beat, but she struggled to keep her voice light. "A couple?"

"Well, yeah." He'd tucked his rain-splattered glasses into his pocket, so the twinkle in the depths of his eyes was easy to see. "There's this cat, you see. We're kind of a package deal."

Maggie nodded slowly. "I'm a package deal, too, you know. Oliver comes with me."

"I know that. In fact, I'm counting on it." He paused a second. "So? What do you think? Are you willing to give this a shot?" He lowered his voice before adding, "Before you answer, fair warning. I'm pretty sure Ruby's on my side."

Maggie laughed shakily. "She definitely is. But—"

His smile dimmed. "But?" he asked gently. "It's okay, Maggie. You should be honest. If you don't think you could…care about me like that—"

"No, it's not that." Maggie's mouth trembled into a shaky smile. "I…already care about you, Neil."

The grin that spread across his face started a warm glow in the pit of her stomach. He was about to kiss her—she could see it in his eyes. She'd better say what she needed to say now. If she didn't, she'd never get the words out.

"But I'm afraid that might not be enough." She could feel her nose starting to run, and she sniffed desperately. "I'm afraid *I* might not be enough."

"Maggie, of course you're—"

"No," she broke in. "Ruby said something earlier that made me realize… I really need to say this. That's the thing about fear. The only way to get rid of it is to drag it out into the open and be honest. If you ignore it, it just grows."

He studied her. "All right. Go ahead and say whatever it is you need to say. I'm listening."

"Thanks." Maggie swallowed hard. "I guess before this goes any further, I need to be sure— really sure—that you understand who I am. And maybe more importantly, who I'm never going to be. You told me Laura was a nurse." She saw Neil start to speak and then restrain himself. "So that means she was smart, like you. That she went to college, like you did. And probably that she was a really great person, too. Most nurses are. Well—" she drew in a deep breath "—I bake cookies for a living, Neil."

"There's nothing wrong with—"

"I know that," Maggie interrupted quickly. "I love my job. That's exactly my point. Baking makes me happy, and that's not going to change. Not only did I not go to college, I never even wanted to go. The minute I walked into Angelo's kitchen, I knew I was right where I wanted to be. The truth is, I'm never going to be as fascinated by history as you are. My bedtime reading consists of cookbooks and romance novels. I've never won an award in my life, and if you take me to a fancy party, I'll probably end up in the kitchen swapping recipes with the caterer. I'm nothing special, Neil. I'm just…me." She shrugged helplessly.

He studied her. "Is that it? Are you finished?"

She blinked. "I guess so."

"Good. Then it's my turn. First off, you're not *just* anything," he said forcefully, his brows drawn together. "As for not being smart, do you know how many idiots have college degrees hanging on their walls? Going to college doesn't make a person smart. Trust me. I've spent plenty of time hanging out with college graduates, and you're one of the most brilliant people I've ever met. Don't give me that look. What about those recipes you're always making up out of thin air? You think everybody can do that? More importantly, you're the kindest person I've ever met. You're generous to a fault, and you're so beautiful—"

Maggie couldn't help it. She sputtered a disbelieving laugh. "Oh, come on."

Neil leaned closer, looking intently into her face. "You *are* beautiful, Maggie, whether you believe it or not. Sometimes when you turn a certain way or smile at me, I…" He shook his head fiercely. "See? I can't even find the words to describe it. Most of the time when you're standing next to me, I can barely catch my breath or remember my own name. Nothing special? You? You're the most special woman I've ever known." He stopped, and his fierce expression shifted into a gentle sadness. "One of the *two* most special women I've ever known," he amended quietly.

"I understand," Maggie started, but he shook his head.

"No, I think it's my turn to be honest now. Laura, our baby…who we were together, it's all part of my past—a part I never want to forget." He rubbed his thumbs gently over her hands. "But the future… That belongs to you and Oliver, if you want it. I really hope you do, because I'm playing for keeps here. I won't rush you. Take whatever time you need, but you might as well know how things stand on my end. I've fallen in love with you, Maggie. I don't expect you to—"

"I love you, too, Neil." Her answer came without conscious thought. Easily. Simply.

Because it was the only answer.

He kissed her then, and the world around them blurred for a few heart-stopping moments. And when her eyes finally fluttered open again, he was looking down at her, his expression dazed.

He started to speak, and she put a finger over his lips.

"Don't say it."

"Don't say what?"

"I know that kiss was pretty amazing, but please don't say *whoa*."

"Okay, I won't." He smiled. "But I'm thinking it."

She sighed and smiled back at him. "So am I." Then she tiptoed and kissed him again.

When they walked into the kitchen a few minutes later, Logan was seated at the table, watching Ruby pour steaming cocoa from a battered saucepan into his mug. As they came through the door, the sheriff's sharp gaze lit on Neil's arm draped possessively around his sister's waist.

"So, that's how it is now," he observed, cocking one eyebrow.

Maggie smiled up at Neil. "That's how it's going to be always," she announced softly.

"Praise the Lord," Ruby said fervently, and then, "Oh, *dear*!" Cocoa had overflowed Logan's mug and was spreading in a brown puddle across the table. The next few minutes were spent mopping up the sticky mess.

"Do you have any idea how much trouble you've caused, Maggie?" Logan grumbled when they'd finally settled back around the table. "Now Ruby's managed to get one of us matched up, she won't be fit to live with."

Ruby beamed as she poured cocoa for Neil and Maggie. "Oh, I can't take credit. The good Lord's behind this, same as every other blessing that comes our way."

"That may be. Still, when you set your mind on something, you're a dangerous woman, Ruby Sawyer," Logan muttered as he sprinkled marshmallows into his cup.

"Not dangerous." His foster mom cocked her head and looked at him speculatively. "Just a little bullheaded, maybe. And of course, I've always been a sucker for the real hard cases. Take you, for instance. You haven't dated anybody for quite a spell, have you, son?"

An alarmed look spasmed across Logan's face. "You leave me out of this."

As Ruby chuckled, a movement caught Maggie's eye. Oliver stood in the doorway in rumpled pajamas, scrubbing his sleepy eyes. "Mama? Neil?"

Maggie's heart went still. *Mama.* He'd never called her that before. She and Neil exchanged looks, and he gave her a wink. "We're right here, sweetie."

Oliver toddled across the worn linoleum, and she lifted him into her lap. "Thunder?"

"That's all over," she reassured him.

The little boy's face relaxed, and he looked around the table with hopeful interest. "Cocoa, Mama? Pwease?"

Ruby was watching him, happy tears puddling in her hazel eyes. "I'll get you some, honey. You just wait right there."

Oliver scooted over in Maggie's lap so that he was closer to Neil and let out a contented sigh. He picked up the marshmallow his uncle Logan rolled in his direction. Ruby fussed over cooling the cocoa with extra milk, testing the temperature carefully before she put it into a sippy cup.

Look at us, Maggie thought joyfully. *We're just like an ordinary family.*

Then she corrected herself. No, not ordinary.

There was nothing ordinary about a family like this. She knew that better than anybody.

Neil leaned close and brushed a kiss against her hair. "Maggie," he whispered in her ear.

She loved the way he said her name. "Yes?"

"I forgot about supper, and I'm starving. You wouldn't happen to have anything to eat around here, would you?"

Maggie laughed. Oliver, not knowing what was so funny, set down his little cup of cocoa and belly laughed with her.

"Sure," she said. "Let me get you a cookie."

Epilogue

A year later, Maggie Hamilton sat in her new minivan, considering the latest house their long-suffering Realtor had suggested.

Neil came around and opened the door. "So? What do you think about this one?"

Maggie used her husband's arm to lever her six-months-pregnant self out onto the gravel driveway. She squinted critically at the pretty home as Neil turned to get Oliver out of his car seat.

"It's beautiful," she admitted. She approved of the deep front porch, the wide windows and the way the sparkling white house sat back off the quiet road, sheltered by towering trees.

"It's not new," Neil warned, "so it's going to need some work. The real-estate agent said the sellers are a married couple in their eighties. They built the house and raised their family here, but now they've moved to be closer to their kids."

"I'm not afraid of work. You know that. But I'm going to need to—"

"—see the kitchen," Neil finished with her. "'The kitchen's the heart of the home,' I know. But please remember, sweetheart—there aren't many properties for sale in Cedar Ridge right now, and this one's the last in our price range. The cabin's already straining at the seams with the three of us. Once the baby gets here—"

Maggie sighed. "I know. And Mrs. Darnell called again this morning, wanting to know when we might be ready to foster. There are so many children needing placements in this area. We need a bigger house, but it has to be the *right* one. Once we start fostering, we won't want to disrupt the kids' lives with a move. If this is it, I'll know." She headed up the brick walkway toward the porch. "Once I see the kitchen."

"Wait up." Neil hurried to walk beside her, Oliver balanced on one arm. He took Maggie's elbow in his other hand. "Mind these steps," he muttered. "The bricks look a little uneven."

Maggie smothered a smile. Neil had been fussing over her ever since she'd discovered her pregnancy four months ago, and he wasn't the only one. Ruby and her brothers and sisters were almost as bad, and Angelo...

Angelo was impossible.

At the wedding, her irritable boss had astonished them by handing over paperwork giving her half ownership in Angelo's. A few months later, when she'd told him about the baby, he'd threatened to take the gift back if she didn't cut her hours and hire more help.

Maggie and Neil wandered arm in arm through the spacious old house as Oliver raced through the echoing rooms. Neil smiled when he saw the expansive living room. "Plenty of room here for the history club to meet," he pointed out.

Maggie laughed. "I'm not so sure. After the stunt you and Logan pulled last week with that World War II tank, Cedar Ridge High is the only school in the state of Georgia where History Club is as popular as the varsity football team."

Neil's smile broadened into a grin. "Not *as* popular," he corrected smugly. "More."

Maggie had to admit, the house *seemed* perfect—so far. It had plenty of bedrooms, generous living areas and pretty country views framed in each window. It was close enough to the school and the bakery and not too far from Ruby, who'd steadfastly refused to consider moving in with the newly married couple. It ticked every single item on the lengthy list she'd drawn up. There was just one last room to check—the most important one.

Maggie was holding her breath as she walked into the kitchen, but as soon as she caught sight of the stove, the air whooshed out of her in a heavy rush. She walked over and touched the elderly appliance with a gentle finger.

"I know," Neil hurried to say. "It's really old. This whole room needs updating. We can paint the cabinets—or I can. You're not getting anywhere near paint for the next few months. And we can move that stove out and replace it with whatever kind you want. Well, within reason. We'll have to budget, but—"

"Are you kidding me? It has two ovens," Maggie said. "*Two*. And six burners. This stove leaves the kitchen over my dead body."

"What?" Hope began to dawn over Neil's face. "Do you mean—?"

"Look at that." Her gaze had caught on a door frame, sporting lots and lots of little scratches, each with a pen-scribbled name over it. She walked over to examine it. "This must be where they kept track of the kids' growth." She opened the door and smiled. It was an old-fashioned pantry, nice and roomy.

She breathed in. Was it her imagination, or could she still smell a whiff of spices in here? Cinnamon, she thought, and maybe a touch of clove.

Neil ran a finger along the scarred door frame. "We could paint over this, I suppose, but it seems a shame. Like erasing a piece of the past." He slanted her a teasing gaze over the top of his glasses. "You probably wouldn't mind that, since you're not a history buff like your husband."

She smiled at him. "I just happen to like making history better than studying it, that's all. There are two sides to this door frame, I notice, and the other one will do fine for measuring our own kids as they grow up. So, what do you say?" She smiled up at her husband. "Feel like making a little history with me in this house, Neil Hamilton?"

He closed the gap between them and kissed her soundly. "You're on," he murmured.

* * * * *

*If you enjoyed this story, don't miss
Laurel Blount's next sweet romance,
available next year from Love Inspired!*

*Find more great reads at
www.LoveInspired.com.*

Dear Reader,

I love a fresh start. Don't you? And I'm especially excited about this one. *Lost and Found Faith* kicks off a brand-new series of books set in Cedar Ridge, a sweet small town nestled in the mountains of north Georgia.

Maggie, Neil and little Oliver's story is such a special one for me because it deals with issues near and dear to my heart. Foster care and adoption have brought some very treasured children into my life. The road isn't always easy—in fact, as Maggie and Oliver can tell us, it's often heartbreakingly difficult. But with faith in God and plenty of love, things sure can work out in amazing ways.

I really hope you've enjoyed visiting Cedar Ridge with me, because I'm planning another trip to this little town soon. Now that Maggie's found her happily-ever-after, Ruby's casting a matchmaking eye toward her oldest foster son, straight-arrow Sheriff Logan Carter. Now, that should be fun to watch—I can't wait!

In the meantime, let's stay in touch! Head over to www.laurelblountbooks.com and sign up to be a part of my favorite bunch of folks—my beloved newsletter subscribers! Every month, I share photos, giveaways, book news and gotta-try-it recipes. And of course, you can always write to me at laurelblountwrites@gmail.com. I look forward to hearing from you!

With love,
Laurel

Get 4 FREE REWARDS!

We'll send you 2 FREE Books plus 2 FREE Mystery Gifts.

Love Inspired books feature uplifting stories where faith helps guide you through life's challenges and discover the promise of a new beginning.

FREE
Value Over
$20

YES! Please send me 2 FREE Love Inspired Romance novels and my 2 FREE mystery gifts (gifts are worth about $10 retail). After receiving them, if I don't wish to receive any more books, I can return the shipping statement marked "cancel." If I don't cancel, I will receive 6 brand-new novels every month and be billed just $5.24 each for the regular-print edition or $5.99 each for the larger-print edition in the U.S., or $5.74 each for the regular-print edition or $6.24 each for the larger-print edition in Canada. That's a savings of at least 13% off the cover price. It's quite a bargain! Shipping and handling is just 50¢ per book in the U.S. and $1.25 per book in Canada.* I understand that accepting the 2 free books and gifts places me under no obligation to buy anything. I can always return a shipment and cancel at any time. The free books and gifts are mine to keep no matter what I decide.

Choose one: ☐ **Love Inspired Romance**
Regular-Print
(105/305 IDN GNWC)

☐ **Love Inspired Romance**
Larger-Print
(122/322 IDN GNWC)

Name (please print)

Address   Apt. #

City   State/Province   Zip/Postal Code

Email: Please check this box ☐ if you would like to receive newsletters and promotional emails from Harlequin Enterprises ULC and its affiliates. You can unsubscribe anytime.

Mail to the **Harlequin Reader Service:**
IN U.S.A.: P.O. Box 1341, Buffalo, NY 14240-8531
IN CANADA: P.O. Box 603, Fort Erie, Ontario L2A 5X3

Want to try 2 free books from another series? Call 1-800-873-8635 or visit www.ReaderService.com.
